"You're safe here," Logan murmured huskily. **"I won't let anything happen to you."**

He lifted a hand and traced a finger down her cheek, leaving shivers behind.

"And who's going to protect you?" Her voice came out sharper than she'd intended, edged with nerves and his unsettling nearness. "When I saw you in the truck…" She bowed her head and found that her forehead rested comfortably on the slope of his chest. "I thought you were dead."

"Hey," he said, nudging a finger beneath her chin to tip her head up. "You don't need to worry about me. It's my job to worry about you."

No, it's not, she wanted to say, *I can take care of myself.* But she said nothing, because she was trapped in his eyes. In the warmth of his body pouring into hers and the inevitable knowledge that he was going to kiss her. That this was all wrong.

And all right.

Then he kissed her, and she couldn't think anymore.

Dear Harlequin Intrigue Reader,

It might be warm outside, but our June lineup will thrill and chill you!

* This month, we have a couple of great miniseries. *Man of Her Dreams* is the spine-tingling conclusion to Debra Webb's trilogy THE ENFORCERS. And there are just two installments left in B.J. Daniels's McCALLS' MONTANA series—*High-Caliber Cowboy* is out now, and *Shotgun Surrender* will be available next month.

* We also have two fantastic special promotions. First, is our Gothic ECLIPSE title, *Mystique*, by Charlotte Douglas. And Dani Sinclair brings you *D.B. Hayes, Detective*, the second installment in our LIPSTICK LTD. promotion featuring sexy sleuths.

* Last, but definitely not least, is Jessica Andersen's *The Sheriff's Daughter*. Sparks fly between a medical investigator and a vet in this exciting medical thriller.

* Also, keep your eyes peeled for Joanna Wayne's THE GENTLEMAN'S CLUB, available from Signature Spotlight.

This month, and every month, we promise to deliver six of the best romantic suspense titles around. Don't miss a single one!

Sincerely,

Denise O'Sullivan
Senior Editor
Harlequin Intrigue

THE SHERIFF'S DAUGHTER

JESSICA ANDERSEN

HARLEQUIN®

TORONTO • NEW YORK • LONDON
AMSTERDAM • PARIS • SYDNEY • HAMBURG
STOCKHOLM • ATHENS • TOKYO • MILAN • MADRID
PRAGUE • WARSAW • BUDAPEST • AUCKLAND

ISBN 0-373-22850-3

THE SHERIFF'S DAUGHTER

ABOUT THE AUTHOR

Though she's tried out professions ranging from cleaning sea lion cages to cloning glaucoma genes, from patent law to training horses, Jessica is happiest when she's combining all these interests with her first love: writing romances. These days she's delighted to be writing full-time on a farm in rural Connecticut that she shares with a small menagerie and a hero named Brian. She hopes you'll visit her at www.JessicaAndersen.com for info on upcoming books, contests and to say "hi"!

Books by Jessica Andersen

CAST OF CHARACTERS

Dr. Samantha Blackwell, DVM—The lady vet has been burned by love before, but she has no real enemies until her new tenant pulls her into his dark, dangerous world.

Dr. Logan Hart, MD—The surgeon-turned-agent is on enforced vacation following a harrowing undercover assignment.

James Donahue—The current town sheriff and a protégé of Sam's retired sheriff father, Jimmy is Sam's good friend—and maybe something more.

Viggo Trehern—The crime boss has been jailed since Logan helped close the net around him. But if Logan is gone, it is likely he will be acquitted.

William Caine—Viggo's right-hand man, Logan would have liked to call him friend. Now he may have to call him executioner.

Dr. Jennifer Lyle, DVM—Sam's partner and good friend, Jen may be in danger by association.

Horace Mann—The head of the local dogfighting community, Horace has little love for Sam, who is a part-time animal officer.

Dr. Sears, DVM—The on-staff vet at the wildly successful racehorse breeding establishment, Bellamy Farms, Sears has no intention of letting Sam near his patients or his livelihood.

Viggo Trehern, Jr.—Viggo Jr. rules the organization in his father's absence. What lengths will he go to in order to see his father returned to power?

Chapter One

A heavy fist pounded on the vet clinic door.

The noise shattered the quiet of the deserted waiting area and Dr. Samantha Blackwell jolted. She shook off sudden unease, tied off one last stitch in the stray dog's sunken hip and raised her voice. "Come on in. It's open!"

There was no answer.

Sam frowned. "Jennifer? Can you get the door?"

Most of her clients knew to let themselves in. The open door policy was standard in Black Horse Beach, even during the just-finished summer months when strangers came and went with the Cape Cod tides. Though Sam was grateful for the income the tourists brought her, she couldn't help resenting that when they left, there were always a few half-grown pets left behind—like the poor dog on her table, whom she'd called Maverick. The crossbred's muzzle and ears bore fighting scars, and the fractures of his ribs and leg told of a run-in with a car.

"Jennifer?" she called again, then shook her head at her own forgetfulness. "Duh. She's in class this morning."

Sam had been too caught up in treating the dog to notice when her partner had taken off for acupuncture class, leaving the clinic empty.

The knock sounded again. Shaking off the creeping heebie-jeebies, which were misplaced since nothing dangerous ever happened in Black Horse Beach, she called out, "Just a minute!"

She picked Maverick up and winced when the pulled muscles in her shoulders and back sparked a protest. She'd been up until dawn delivering an overlarge colt at posh Bellamy Farms. Though the thoroughbred racing stable wasn't a regular client, their live-in vet had been out of town and the mare hadn't been in any mood to wait.

Neither was the person at the door. The knock came again, faster and louder this time, and Sam's heart picked up a beat as adrenaline pushed aside the unaccountable nerves.

It must be an emergency with one of her clients.

"Coming!" She slid Maverick's limp form into one of the lower recovery cages. He'd wake up over the next hour or so, and should survive the broken leg and cracked ribs. Hopefully, during that time she could also repair his failed trust in human beings and find him a new home.

Hurrying now, Sam stripped off her gloves, tossed them into the wood-framed biohazard bin just inside exam room 1 and jogged across the waiting room. She yanked open the door. "I'm here. What's the problem?"

The wooden porch was deserted, but her already unsteady heart thumped double-time when she saw her tenant halfway up the clamshell walkway.

He froze mid-step, lifted his eyes to stare at her, and said, "Problem?"

In the three weeks since she'd rented Beach Plum Cottage to Dr. Logan Hart, she'd tried not to think about the brooding, too handsome M.D. But the moment their gazes connected, she knew she'd been unsuccessful. Like it or not, his eyes haunted her. Light hazel, almost pale gold, they were made striking by a dark brown ring around each iris.

Hunter's eyes, her sheriff father would have called them. Then he would have taken the measure of the man before making a call on his character. But Sam hadn't given Hart the benefit of consideration. There was something…unnerving about him. He was too big, too masculine.

Too much like Travis and Brent. After one divorce and one near miss, Sam had sworn off big, masculine men forever. Which was just as well, since Logan Hart hadn't shown any indication that he wanted to be friends with her—hell, with anyone in town. He kept to himself, sometimes disappearing for days, sometimes holing up in the little cottage for just as long.

Not that Sam had been keeping tabs on him. But since the cottage and her place were the only two structures on Dune Buggy Road, it was hard to miss his comings and goings.

Honest.

Because she was rattled, and because her foolish heart stuttered at the sight of him, Sam squared her shoulders. "You could have come on in. You didn't need to knock so many times."

His long, muscular legs carried him onto the porch, and a frown darkened his habitually guarded expression. "I didn't knock."

"Well, someone did." Sam forced herself not to step away, because that would be retreating, and Sheriff Bob's daughter didn't retreat. Even though her father had long retired to Arizona, she still measured her actions against his expectations. So she stood her ground and stared at the man opposite her.

In his midthirties, Logan Hart was a few years older than she. His dark brown hair caught the fading late-summer sun to glow reddish at the ends, and his worn jeans and black T-shirt showcased his large, powerful frame.

He shook his head. "It wasn't me." His tone brooked no argument, reminding her of the forceful personality she'd glimpsed before, when he'd rented the cottage and pushed for her assurance that he wouldn't be disturbed.

At the time, she'd noted the tense set of his shoulders and the lines of exhaustion in his face and figured he needed to escape a draining medical practice. Now, sensing a faint aura of danger hovering over him, she pressed her back against the molding around the old wooden door and wondered if there was more to him than she'd thought.

"Then it must have been kids," she said, though her gut thought otherwise. What was going on here? "Were you looking for me? Is anything wrong with the cottage?"

"Nothing's wrong with the cottage." Logan's voice was clipped and Yankee, his accent one of expensive Boston schools rather than the softer, flatter cadences of the Cape Cod beach towns. "I came by to drop off the key to your cottage. I'm leaving."

Sam's stomach dropped. Leaving? He couldn't leave. She needed the rental income. Spurred by near panic, she stepped forward and got in his face—well, as close as she could get, given that he topped her by a good six inches. "You can't leave now. You leased the cottage for six more weeks. I have a contract!"

And the money was already spent on new cages and supplies for the no-kill shelter she ran as part of her duties with the Black Horse Animal Protection Agency. The few thousand dollars he'd paid to lease the cottage for nine weeks past-season had been a much-needed windfall.

She wasn't giving the money back. No way.

But Logan held up his hands, tension and an edgy sense of barely-leashed energy etching his powerful arms. He glanced from side to side, then lowered his voice. "Don't worry about the money—it's yours. But I need to get out of town. It's not safe for me—"

A gunshot split the late summer air.

Sam's heart lodged in her throat even as her mind struggled to grasp the words *not safe.*

"Down! Get down!" Logan reacted before she did. He pushed her to the porch and covered her body with his as a second shot hit the brass plaque that advertised her hours. The sign chimed like an off-tune bell.

"Get off!" Panicked, Sam pushed at him and struggled to escape even as she heard two more shots.

"Go!" He rolled to one side and shoved her toward the clinic. "Call 911."

A fifth shot plowed into the porch between them. Pain flared as a splinter of wood pierced her jeans and dug into her hip. "Someone's shooting at us!"

"Get in the house and stay there." Though his eyes were hard, his voice was controlled, as though people shot at him every day. But that made no sense. He was a *doctor.*

Wasn't he?

Oh, God. Who had she rented the cottage to? What if he was some sort of criminal? She'd done a routine credit check, but what if—?

Heart pounding, she scrambled backward on her hands and rear end, eyes glued across the road on the high scrub brush that screened a small estuary from view.

When she realized where the shots were coming from, she stiffened. "It could be hunters," she whispered into a moment of silence. "Poachers. They're not supposed to shoot over there, but they do sometimes."

They'd even blasted out the back window of her vet's van once. But that didn't account for her tenant's quick, practiced reaction or the dark anger in his eyes.

"Maybe." In a smooth motion, he dropped down off the porch and crouched in the shadows behind a spreading rhododendron. He turned back to her and growled, "Stay there."

"Wait!" She grabbed for his arm but missed when the splinter in her hip protested. "What the hell is going on? Who *are* you?"

He frowned, eyes narrowed with irritation, or maybe guilt. "I'll be gone soon—that's all you need to know."

With that, he slipped from the rhododendron to the side of his truck, then ran lightly across the road toward the estuary. He dove into the bushes, which snapped together in his wake.

Then there was silence.

Sam wasted little time on debate; she was her father's daughter, after all. She darted into the clinic, yanked the double-barreled shotgun from behind the office door, grabbed a handful of cartridges from the desk, and scooped up her cell phone. Her hands shook as she punched in the three digits.

"Nine-one-one," a familiar, perky voice said in her ear. "What's your emergency?"

"Treece, it's Sam. I need you to send Jimmy out here right away."

The dispatcher's voice sharpened to serious in an instant. "What's wrong?"

"I'm not sure." Sam wiped a sweaty palm against her jean-clad leg. "Either the poachers are at it again over in the estuary, or my tenant is in some sort of danger."

She had a suspicion it was the latter. No wonder she'd found him attractive. Her hormones always leaned toward trouble.

"Where will you be?"

Sam took a deep breath and swallowed hard. "Tell Jimmy I'll meet him near the water." She folded the phone shut, cutting Treece off midprotest. Then she hefted the shotgun, ignored the stitch in her hip and limped across the road.

Logan Hart needed help and she was the only one around to give it right then.

Besides, she had her daddy's shotgun.

STUPID. Logan cursed himself as he pushed through the thick, screening brush. He'd been stupid to think Viggo Trehern's men wouldn't follow him here. And because of his stupidity, his pretty landlady had been endangered. His fault.

The silence of the nearby woods told him the shooters were long gone, but that didn't help matters. They'd be back. They couldn't afford to leave him alive.

The case Logan and his employers at Hospitals for Humanity—HFH—had helped build against Trehern was solid. The feds had failed to convict the crime boss on charges ranging from extortion to murder, but HFH had managed to get him indicted on a lesser federal crime. For the past six-plus years, the leader of the unholy Boston-based syndicate had fed his prescription drug habit with a combination of illegal doctor shopping and sidewalk deals. The case Logan and his team had developed was a lock.

Or so it had seemed. But just that day, Trehern's lawyers had earned their Armanis by delaying the trial yet again. Logan might have wondered why, except for the glare Trehern had fixed on him as the guards had led the older man away. It had promised revenge against Logan, who had gone undercover, penetrated Trehern's circle of trust and gathered the damning evidence.

He had understood the look with a flash of intuition and a sharp slice of worry.

Trehern had put out a contract on him.

Now, as the ghosts of gunshots echoed in his ears, he thought, *Damn. Viggo's men move fast.*

He pushed through the last of the clinging thorn bushes and emerged at the edge of a lake, or maybe a finger of brackish water from the nearby Atlantic. There was no sign of the shooter—or shooters—but footprints marred the soft edge of the water and spent casings gleamed on the sand, their aura of death reminding him of the fourteen months he'd spent as Trehern's confidante.

Reminding him of the things he'd seen, and hoped never to see again.

Brush rustled to his left. He spun and grabbed for his gun, but he'd left the .44 behind at the cottage, thinking he had time enough to pick up his things and run for the city, where his employers could keep him safe. He hadn't wanted to carry a weapon in this peaceful town, just as he'd hoped the violence wouldn't follow him.

Bad call.

Footsteps crashed and Logan faded behind a nearby tree as a shadowy human figure emerged, gun barrel first.

He seized the shotgun, yanked forward and down, and grabbed the gunman by the throat. In the instant it took him to spin the figure around and press it against a nearby tree, two things happened.

His brain told him it was a woman.

His body told him it was Samantha Blackwell, with her strawberry-blond hair, blue eyes and knockout figure.

He swallowed hard and forced himself not to move closer.

HUNTER'S EYES, was all Sam could think in that first moment when Logan pressed her against a tree with a forearm across her throat. Those eyes loomed large in her vision, amber and dark-rimmed and molten with barely suppressed violence. His legs tangled with hers, their bodies bumped at thigh and chest and she froze when heat flared through her, composed of equal parts fear and sexual awareness.

His eyes locked on hers, then blurred with recognition. He jerked away and she nearly collapsed in shocked relief. Only then did the fear take over.

What had she been thinking? She'd run toward the bullets, crashed into a blind situation, with nothing but a—

"Damn it, woman." Logan leaned close, face tight with anger and something else. "I told you to stay inside the clinic!"

Though she knew she'd been wrong, Sam's hard-learned bravery forced her to snap back, "And leave you over here alone? No way. Those hunters might have been drunk. Don't you know how dangerous it is to go into a firing zone?"

"Of course I do!" he shouted. "That's my damn job!"

"You're a doctor, not an entire SWAT team!" The squeal of tires on dirt and gravel jolted them both, until Jimmy's familiar voice hailed them from the road.

"Sam? You okay in there? You find the poachers?"

Not wanting to analyze the unsteady thump of her heart or the tension that was nearly visible in the air around her and Logan, Sam answered her childhood friend and current…well, she honestly wasn't sure what Sheriff Jimmy Donahue was to her at this point. Especially not after the lightning bolt that had slashed through her body when Logan crowded her up against the tree. "We're over here, Jimmy. And no, we didn't find the shooter."

Brush crashed nearby and Sam stepped away from Logan, though she couldn't have said why. Moments later, Jimmy appeared, walking carefully and fanning his weapon in a neat arc. His tan uniform hung slightly askew on his lanky frame, and he'd ditched his official hat for a Red Sox cap again.

James Donahue had grown from an earnest, fair-haired boy into a loyal, strong-willed man who would, by his own admission, do pretty much anything Sam wanted him to. Their friendship was a comfort. Recently, he'd been pushing for more, but she hadn't been sure how to respond. Part of her wanted the safety and steadiness he represented, so different from her past experiences.

But another part of her craved flash and the flame, and the sexual delirium that never seemed to go hand in hand with safety and steadiness.

No, it came from the men who were bad for her, the ones who didn't stay put, didn't slow down. She was a confirmed sucker for that sort. Because of it, and because she'd vowed not to put herself through the pain again, she edged even farther away from Logan as Jimmy joined them.

The sheriff glanced at her, brow furrowed. "You okay?" He turned to Logan. "You're the tenant, right?"

Used to Jimmy's habit of carrying on multiple conversations at once, Sam nodded and answered both questions. "Yes, he's renting the cottage. And yes, I'm fine." She brushed at her hip, which stung like fire. "Though I think I caught a splinter."

That was when she looked down and saw the blood.

The men followed her gesture and Logan swore inventively. "Damn it, woman, the bullet must have creased you!"

The pain came then, swooping down on Sam as though it had been waiting for her to notice. It vised her head and hip and sent her reeling back against the tree that his virile male body had pressed her into mere minutes earlier.

Shot. She'd been shot. Oh, hell. The cadence of the words beat through her with the tempo of her heart, but it didn't sweep away the sight of Logan's eyes, or the flash of guilt deep within them. The sight reminded her of the words *not safe,* and of the professional way he'd slid off the porch and double-timed it across the road toward danger.

As he came toward her, she leaned against the tree and looked up into his hard-set eyes. "What the hell just happened here?"

His lips tightened on an oath, or maybe an apology. She could see both in his eyes. "It doesn't matter. I'll take it with me when I go—and I'm out of here as soon as we get you patched up."

With that, he scooped her up into his arms as though he had every right, and carried her away from the estuary. Away from the bright glitter of rifle shell casings.

She struggled against his iron-hard grip. "Put me down. I can walk!"

"You're bleeding," he replied calmly, the dark rumble of his voice resonating from deep within his chest. "And whatever else I've been, I'm a doctor first and foremost."

She half expected Jimmy to demand that Logan put her down, but the sheriff's attention was focused elsewhere. He crouched down near the footprints and frowned, then looked up at her. Their eyes met over Logan's shoulder.

In his face she read the truth she had feared, and her stomach clenched into a fist.

The shots had been deliberately aimed at her house.

Someone had tried to kill Logan Hart on her front porch.

Chapter Two

The lady vet was a handful in more ways than one, but Logan's mind wasn't on the curvy bundle of woman he carried up the narrow stairs to her apartment over the clinic, or on the stubborn daring that had sent her across the road after him. No, he was focused on the salty smell of fresh blood and the seeping stain on the torn jeans just below her waistband.

The wound wasn't fatal. Probably wasn't more than a shallow crease. But that didn't stop his brain from showing him images of a pretty blonde with a bullet hole through her forehead and most of the back of her head blown away.

Sharilee Winters.

He'd thought her one of Trehern's women and despised her for it. He'd found out too late that she was undercover just as deep as him, working for an offshoot of the federal government that wasn't accountable to any of the other branches involved in the operation.

Afterward, when Logan had asked for the group's name, the others had looked away. When he'd asked how to reach Sharilee's family, he had received vague mumbles and disconnected numbers. So he'd been left to remember her face and her death and wonder who mourned her loss.

In the six long months since Trehern had been jailed, Logan had almost convinced himself he couldn't have stopped the bastard from executing Sharilee. He'd almost convinced himself his reflexes hadn't been slowed by his belief that Sharilee was nothing more than a hooker, or by his vague notion that Trehern's right-hand man, William Caine, was an undercover operative, that he would help if things went south before the sting.

But Sharilee had been the operative, not William. And she had died horribly for her work. For justice.

"Logan?" Sam's voice recalled him to the present, to the new guilt. The shooter had come for him, not her. He needed to get out, and get out fast. His employers had a high-security apartment set aside for him in the city, where he could stay until the trial resumed later that week.

Let Trehern's goons *try* to get him there.

"We'll get you fixed up in no time," he said, falling back on a surgeon's platitudes when nothing else made sense. When he got no response, he looked down at the woman in his arms. A quiver of surprise ran through his body when he found her eyes open and alert.

And focused on his face.

A second tremor worked its way through his body, this one hotter than surprise.

More urgent, and unexpected for its power.

When he reached the living area of her small apartment, he set her on her feet, afraid that if he carried her into the bedroom and lowered her to the rumpled bed he glimpsed through a half-open door, he might act on the ideas that had been flitting through his skull with annoying regularity since he'd first rented her cottage.

Take a few months off, his bosses had said. *Remember what it's like to be you.* Zachary Cage, his immediate superior at the Boston General branch of Hospitals for Humanity, had even gone so far as to lift an eyebrow and suggest that Logan have a fling.

But he barely knew what it was like to be *him* anymore, and he had no stomach for flings—or relationships, for that matter. His low-grade interest in happily-ever-after had been shot to hell three months ago when his sister Nancy's husband had gone overseas on HFH orders and never come home. Her teary-eyed vigil while she waited for word of Stephen's fate had reconfirmed what Logan had learned during his eighteen months undercover.

It wasn't fair for a man in his business to love a woman, to have a family. It had torn Nancy to pieces when Logan had gone under for that year and a half, and to lose her husband so soon after had been nearly a crushing blow.

He'd juggled the trial as best he could, and spent time with her when she let him, waiting. Hoping. But as the days passed, then weeks, hope had begun to fade, and with it his sister. These days, she was hanging on to optimism by her fingernails, rejecting the other option.

Love just wasn't worth it, Logan had decided. It wasn't worth the pain of the one left behind. And he was too old, too jaded for the temporary affairs the younger members of HFH indulged in between assignments. So even though attraction had sizzled through him the moment he'd first seen his new landlady, he'd stayed away and banished her from his thoughts when her image sneaked back in.

At least he'd tried.

But now, standing a breath away from her, conscious of the rise and fall of her breasts beneath the blue-patterned vet's smock, he realized he'd failed. She'd been at the edges of his thoughts all along.

And that was a complication he didn't have the time or the heart for. Not now.

So he focused on her bloodstained hip. The best thing he could do for her was to treat her and get the hell out of Black Horse Beach. He gestured toward the shallow crease, which had stopped bleeding. "You want me to take a look at that, or would you rather manage it yourself?"

He hadn't spent much time in the small beachfront town, but the few conversations he'd had with the locals all came back to his landlady somehow. The year-round inhabitants of Black Horse Beach saw her as a cross between Dr. Dolittle and Florence Nightingale. In the space of ten minutes at a coffee shop one morning, he'd learned about her work with the local animal protection agency, her spay-a-stray program, and her father, the former sheriff.

Logan had no doubt from the conversations that Dr. Blackwell could treat her own hip if she wanted, but the pale, blue-eyed woman standing opposite him looked little like the invincible picture the neighbors had painted of her.

She looked fragile. And tired. And hurting.

The last, at least, was his fault.

"Go on." He nudged her toward the small bathroom he saw off the narrow hallway that separated her teacup-sized living room from the modern-looking kitchen. "You change into something loose while I run down to my truck and get my field kit, okay?" When she merely stared at him, he gentled his voice. "It won't hurt, I promise." Foolish words, empty words, he thought to himself. Of course it would hurt. She'd been nicked by a bullet meant for him.

But still, she didn't move. Finally, she reached out a steady hand and touched his cheek. He nearly flinched at the spark of contact and the compassion in her voice when she said, "Please tell me who you are. Why aren't you safe? Why was someone shooting at you? Tell me. Maybe we can help."

Startled by her calm and by her offer of help to a stranger who'd nearly gotten her killed, he stared back at her for a moment. The urge to tell her everything warred with the need to get the hell out of town, forming a messy ball of unease in his chest. The former won out because part of him didn't want her thinking he was a criminal, even if it had been his miscalculation that had brought the shooters to her doorstep.

He shoved his hands in his pockets. "I work for a group of medical investigators called HFH. Earlier this year, we helped bust Viggo Trehern."

Her quick indrawn breath and the flash of comprehension in her eyes told him she knew some of the story. "That was you?"

"In part." In large part, but she didn't need to know how large. "Now he's up on trial, and it looks like he's decided to win the old-fashioned way. By killing the witnesses."

This time her gasp was louder, but she mastered the reaction quickly, and a hint of relief crept into her vivid eyes. "Then you work for the government. You're one of the good guys."

Technically, it was true, but eighteen months in Trehern's world had marked him. He was harder than he'd been when he went in. Less certain of right and wrong, less willing to deal with the necessary shades of gray.

And even though he'd told her about HFH to prove that he wasn't one of the bad guys, Logan couldn't bring himself to claim the alternative.

Hell, he wasn't sure *what* he was anymore. And that, more than anything, had prompted the bosses to give him this enforced time off. Time to figure it out. Time to decide.

Time to heal.

Because he hadn't figured it out or decided, and because the scar tissue on his soul wasn't even close to set, he stepped forward until he could feel the warmth of her body against his skin. She leaned back slightly and her pupils widened a fraction with nerves, though she still didn't look scared enough for his purposes.

"Dr. Blackwell," he said quietly, "you have no idea what I am. So I'd suggest that you let me patch up your hip so I can get the hell out of your town before something worse than a shooter comes looking for me. Do you understand what I'm saying?"

She surprised him by lifting her chin. "Yes. I understand."

But when she turned and limped toward the tiny bathroom, Logan was left with the feeling that what he'd meant and what she'd understood had been two very different things.

And what the hell was he going to do about that?

The door closed with a final-sounding thud. Logan muttered a curse and headed for the stairs. A few four-by-four gauze pads and he was out of there.

In the city, with HFH backup, he could lure Trehern's men into a trap. Here, he could do nothing but involve innocent bystanders.

Jimmy Donahue met him at the bottom of the stairs wearing a scowl edged with worry. The sheriff stood with his shoulders braced, his arms folded across his chest. Tall and lean, maybe a year or two younger than Logan, he wasn't physically overwhelming, but Logan sensed a core of strength that told him the sheriff wasn't a man to be underestimated. Jimmy frowned and asked, "She's going to be okay, right?"

Logan nodded. "Yeah, she'll be fine. Barely a scar. I just need to grab my field kit from the truck."

The sheriff followed. "Does the shooting have to do with the Trehern trial?" At Logan's startled look, Jimmy shrugged. "We *do* have cable Internet down here, you know."

"And you look up every stranger who comes to town?"

"Nope. Only the ones who rent from Sam."

Only the thirty-something, seemingly unattached men who rented from Samantha, Logan guessed, figuring that number was pretty small. This was a family-and-beach-ball sort of place, not a singles' retreat.

He glanced over, wondering whether Samantha and the sheriff were an item and knowing he shouldn't care. "How much do you know?"

"I know that Viggo Trehern is scum." Jimmy's glare told Logan the only reason he scored better was his opposition to the murdering crime boss. "And I know it's a damn shame the only thing they could nail him on was buying a boatload of prescriptions from dirty doctors."

"Capone was put in Alcatraz for tax evasion when nothing else would stick," Logan pointed out as he reached into his truck and pulled out his HFH field kit.

"That doesn't make it right. Anyway, I couldn't get as much information as I would've liked, but you're listed as one of the expert witnesses. Something about medical investigations."

"I'm impressed you got that far. That data is supposed to be buried deep."

"It was." Jimmy met his eyes, a faint smile tipping the corners of his mouth. "Just because we're not big city, big hospital doesn't mean we don't have…skills." Then his expression hardened. "Tell me what I need to know about the shooter."

His tone brooked no argument.

Quickly adjusting his first impression of the local law, Logan turned back to the clinic and tried to decide whether the prickle at the back of his neck was a guilty conscience or watching eyes. "Shooter? Just one?"

The sheriff nodded and matched him stride for stride. "Yeah, one set of footprints. One set of casings."

That seemed odd. Trehern left little to chance, so Logan would have expected a backup shooter. Then again, he would have expected them to hit what they were aiming at. The bullets had come close, but not close enough.

How had the assassin missed? More importantly, why?

They reached the clinic and pushed through into the waiting room. Knowing the sheriff wasn't done with him yet, Logan paused and turned to the other man. "I'll head back to the city after I doctor her wound. Get myself put in protective custody." Technically, it would be HFH protection, but the sheriff didn't need to know that. The Investigations Division tried to keep a low profile to the non-medical types. "I'll make it real obvious I'm going, so there won't be any question in the minds of Viggo's goons."

The sheriff considered for a moment, then nodded. "It's probably best if you leave." Logan didn't think they were talking about the shooter anymore. Jimmy's quick glance to the stairway confirmed the suspicion, as did his next words. "Sam doesn't need any more drama in her life."

Logan didn't care. He couldn't care. But he found himself asking, "What drama?"

"Her mother up and left when she was in grade school, said she couldn't live in such a pissant town married to the local sheriff. Sam's daddy raised her, but damned if she hasn't paired off with a couple of tough guys just like him except for one thing—they don't treat her right." Jimmy shot him a sidelong glance. "I wouldn't be telling you this if I hadn't seen the way you two were looking at each other in the woods."

Logan remembered the moment. It was burned in his brain. Under his skin. When he'd pushed her up against that tree, the man in him had howled at the feel of soft curves and the smell of warm woman even as the undercover operative in him had identified her as friend, not foe. He could have moved away sooner, but he hadn't wanted to.

He pushed the memory aside and found the sheriff watching him with knowing eyes. Because of it, and because guilt pricked his conscience, Logan bristled.

"Consider me warned off, Sheriff. I'll be gone before you know it, leaving the field clear."

Jimmy merely inclined his head. "All right, then. Come by my office on your way out of town."

He couldn't have been any clearer if he'd said, *Wave, so I know you're really gone.* But Logan couldn't fault him, either as a sheriff or a man.

He'd do the same if Samantha were his.

SAM PAUSED AT THE TOP of the stairs and heard the low rumble of male voices. The sound brought her back to the days of living with each of her exes, of not being alone in the evenings. The stinging throb of her hip echoed the pounding in her head and she impatiently brushed away a tear, blaming it on shock and delayed reaction.

She'd been shot at. She deserved to have the shakes. Worse, as she'd changed clothes and bandaged the shallow slice herself with gauze and ointment from the bathroom cabinet, she'd realized they had overlooked something important.

The shots might not have been aimed at Logan.

She limped down the stairs. The voices grew louder then stopped abruptly as the men became aware of her. The tension in the air suggested their conversation had not been entirely friendly. Jimmy's guilty look told Sam that she'd been the subject, but she had more important things to worry about. So she crossed her arms and focused on Logan, who regarded her with cool, hooded eyes.

"Remember when I opened the door and accused you of knocking? Well, if it wasn't you, then *someone* knocked on the clinic door three separate times before you arrived. If that was meant to get me to open the door, then…"

She couldn't bring herself to say it aloud, but the darkening of Logan's expression was answer enough.

She could have been the target.

Outside, the sun had set. Though the late summer evening was warm, a chill cut through her long-sleeved shirt and the loose drawstring pants she'd pulled over the neat four-by-four bandage she'd slapped over the stinging cut on her hip. Goose bumps rose at Logan's quiet curse and she rubbed her arms to smooth the fine hairs.

"That doesn't make any sense." Jimmy looked from one to the other of them. "Sam doesn't have any enemies. Nobody would want to shoot her!"

His words seemed to come from far away. She was trapped in Logan's eyes, focused entirely on a man she'd met only three weeks earlier. Her hormones reacted to him like he was one of the he-men she'd vowed to avoid, but his actions so far marked him as a good guy. Still, he wasn't the sort to stick around—he'd said so himself.

He was on his way out of town, never to return.

"Is that true, Samantha?" His voice spanned the gap between them and seemed to brush her lips with a feathery caress. "You have no enemies? What about your exes?"

Ouch. She shot Jimmy a glare, knowing exactly how and why Logan had learned about Travis and Brent.

"The partings were amicable." Both of them. "There's no reason they would want me dead. No shared property, no continuing financial connections. Nada."

If her love hadn't been enough to keep the men in town, it sure as hell wasn't enough to incite murderous jealousy.

Besides, she and Louie had split two years earlier. The most action she'd gotten since was when eighty-year-old Art Furnace winked at her in the grocery store over a rack of melons.

Small-town living was hell on a social life. But she loved just about everything else about it, especially the differences she could make on her own level.

Jimmy's radio squawked on his belt as Treece's voice was distorted by the signal strength and tinny speakers. The sheriff held up a hand. "I'll be right back."

He answered his dispatcher on the way out the door and stood on the front porch for her report, perhaps for privacy, perhaps for a better signal.

But the upshot was that he left Sam alone with Logan. The walls seemed to press closer, the air to thicken. His eyes were intent on her, and she sensed that he wanted to ask about her exes. But instead, he said, "What about your father? A former sheriff must have some enemies."

For someone who'd seemed to avoid her almost as carefully as she'd avoided him for the past few weeks, Logan sure seemed to know a whole lot about her, whereas she knew nearly nothing about him.

"None that I know of." Suddenly needing to do something, anything, Sam turned away blindly and limped toward the back room. The stray dog's injuries and recovery from anesthesia gave her an excuse to leave the waiting room, a reason not to stand opposite Logan and wonder what he was thinking.

He caught her arm. "Your hip. I'm sorry, I forgot. Let me look at it."

"It's fine. I slapped some Betadine and a bandage on it, and took a few aspirin." She pulled away, hating that her body buzzed in reaction at his touch. Though he might technically work on the side of justice, his closed demeanor and dark broodiness screamed trouble, and she was avoiding trouble these days. "It'll be sore for a few days, but there was more blood than real damage. Just a scratch. Don't worry about it."

He followed her into the recovery area, where three of the twelve cages were occupied by patients, the rest by rescued strays. "I do worry about it, damn it. You wouldn't have been hurt if it wasn't for me. Whether or not someone knocked first, I was the target, period."

"Then why did they knock?" She opened Maverick's cage door and touched the stray dog's sunken yellow flank. She half hoped for a tail wag or a lick of appreciation. Instead, she got a vicious growl.

Maverick would need time and love before he believed that things were different now. His life was different now.

Or it could be, if he learned to trust her.

"I don't know." Logan turned away from her and pulled a hand through his short brown hair. "It makes no sense, unless—"

He broke off as Jimmy rejoined them. The sheriff's expression was moody, nearly matching Logan's threatening scowl. A shiver crawled across Sam's skin. "Unless what?"

"Unless they've targeted you because of your association with me." Logan cursed and strode back out into the waiting room. He opened the front door and glared out, though the moonless night was impenetrably black.

She followed, unsettled by the tension in his powerful frame and the idea that a Boston crime boss would want to kill her. "What association? I rented you a cottage, nothing more."

Viggo Trehern had no way of knowing she'd entertained more than a few fantasies about her handsome tenant.

"That's the way he works." Logan stared out into the night, one hand pressed against the door frame, inches above a raw wood scar where a bullet had gouged through the molding. "I was undercover in his operation for more than a year and a half. Trust me. I know how he works. Even the slightest association, the slightest sign of interest is enough for him to take notice. We've seen to it that my parents and sister are safe, so he might have gone looking for another target. You."

The hollow guilt in Logan's voice sent Sam forward a step, but Jimmy's hand on her arm held her back.

"There's more," the sheriff said in a low, urgent tone that focused her attention instantly.

"What?" Sam said, "Did someone find the shooter?" Against all logic, she felt a spurt of hope that it had been nothing more than a poacher with rotten aim.

Jimmy shook his head. "No, but Edna's grandson found a rifle on the beach below Third Cliff. It looks like someone threw it off the top figuring to hit the water, but misjudged the tide. Or maybe it washed up. I need to go take a look."

Logan frowned. "You can't send someone else?"

"No." The sheriff shrugged uncomfortably. "This is a small community. I've got two part-timers, but they're both off at a conference until the day after tomorrow. I'm it until then."

The men traded a look and Sam was unsurprised when Logan said, "I'll stay here and keep watch."

"I thought you were leaving." She crossed her arms and ignored the goose bumps that threatened to rise again, though she glanced at the shotgun Logan had leaned beside the door, gaining an obscure comfort from its nearness.

"Not if they're trying to get to me through you." He returned his attention to the dark night. "If that's the case, my leaving won't protect you."

The flat pronouncement sent a quiver through her stomach, and she suddenly wished someone would hold her and tell her everything was going to be okay. She wasn't usually shaky or squeamish, but this had been anything but a normal day.

She could use a hug.

But Jimmy was already halfway out the door and she knew for a fact that touching Logan was like tweaking a live wire. A moment of electric shock and a lingering moment of sizzle.

She'd learned her lesson about shock and sizzle. It didn't last. So she turned away. "I'm going to bed my patients down for the night. When you're ready, lock the front door and come upstairs. I'll make us some dinner."

She didn't bother trying to convince him she was fine on her own. For one, she didn't think it would work. And for another, she didn't want to be alone.

But she wasn't sure he was the best choice of company, either. She was too aware of him standing silent sentinel as she medicated Maverick and the other patients, then fed the shelter residents. When she went upstairs, he locked up and followed silently, carrying her father's shotgun like an extension of his body. All the while, she knew where he was at every moment, as though she could hear him breathe, feel the pulse of blood through his veins.

"Burgers okay?" she asked once she gained the relative safety of her small kitchen.

"Fine." He leaned the shotgun against the wall. "Can I help?"

"No, you sit. This kitchen is barely big enough for me, never mind for two." She busied herself in the fridge and heard him step toward the kitchen door.

"I'm going to make a few calls," he said, and slipped out into the hall as though he was equally unsettled by the tension that buzzed in the air between them.

It wasn't until she came close to cutting her thumb off that Sam realized her fingers were shaking. She put down the knife and the wedge of cheese and held up her hands. At the sight of their trembles, tears pressed against her eyelids and the slice on her hip stung a protest, pushing the tears harder.

What was the matter with her? She'd been in danger before. As an animal-control officer, she'd had dogs sicced on her and guns waved in her face. Horace Mann, the head of the local illegal dogfighting community, had even attacked her once. She'd beaten him off with her control stick, a lightweight aluminum pole with a retractable cable at one end. Normally used to control feral dogs and cats, it had been barely enough to fend off Horace, who'd blasted at her with his shotgun as she'd peeled away from his deceptively neat home.

So why was she so shaken now?

Because, she realized, this wasn't Horace, and it wasn't part of Black Horse Beach. This was a danger from outside, something bigger than their little area was used to.

And then there was Logan Hart. It would be dishonest of her to pretend the shakes were all from shock or fear. There was a good dose of excitement mixed through the nerves, courtesy of the big man whose very presence overwhelmed her small set of rooms.

Damning the part of her that wanted to be a fool all over again, she resolutely picked up the cheese and the knife.

She just had to get through the next day and a half safely, then Jimmy's part-timers would be back from their convention and Logan would be free to take himself out of Black Horse Beach and back to the city, where his people could convict Trehern and he could get back to his life.

Because that was what men like Logan did. They went on with their lives.

OUT IN SAMANTHA'S LIVING ROOM, Logan paced the small space with his cell to his ear while Zach Cage's voice gave him the bad news.

Or not bad news, precisely. Confusing news. Information that didn't fit into his hypothesis.

Logan frowned. "So if William, Martin Gross and the others are all accounted for, then who did Viggo send down here?" He could almost say the names now without flinching, without immediately picturing the things he'd seen the evil men do. The things he'd been unable to stop because he'd needed to establish a seamless cover.

"Beats me," Cage answered, and Logan heard frustration in the words. HFH was worried about the trial, about the delays and about the shooting in Black Horse Beach. "Would Trehern hire outside help?"

"Not Viggo," Logan answered. "He likes to keep his dirty work close."

"But if he's not running the operation anymore, if

someone else is calling the shots…" Cage trailed off, not needing to finish the thought, which chilled Logan's guts instantly with its logic.

If Trehern's operation was being run by one of his lieutenants—either cold-blooded William Caine, or his son Viggo Jr.—then all bets were off. In fact, that made it far more likely that the hit had been contracted outside the organization.

To professional killers.

After a moment, Logan's boss exhaled noisily. "I don't like this. I want you back in the city, pronto, locked down in the apartment building with guards and guns, at least for the next three days, until the trial resumes."

"I can't do that, boss." Though a large part of him wished he could, not because he was afraid for himself, but because he longed to draw the killers into the city, away from Black Horse Beach. Away from Samantha.

"Why not? Because of the woman?"

The woman in question stuck her head out of the kitchen. "Burgers are ready. You want to eat in here?" Her expression was the same mix of hope and dread he felt in his own chest.

He wanted to share a meal with her. But at the same time, he knew it was a bad idea. So he held up the phone, aware that Cage still waited on the line. "I've got more calls to make. Can you fix me a plate to take downstairs?"

Let her think the calls were private, though it was more that he couldn't afford to spend time with her. He didn't dare, because already the sexual tension hummed in the air between them, unseen and unacknowledged, but impossible to ignore.

When she nodded with a flash of something like relief in her eyes, then disappeared into the kitchen, he held the phone back up to his ear.

"That her?" Cage asked.

"Yeah. That's her." The words rang truer than he liked.

"What are you going to do?"

"Tomorrow, I'm going to do my best to find the shooter," Logan vowed. "It'd help if you sent me a couple of bodies."

"I'll do my best, though we're short-handed at the moment. We've got something big going on overseas." Before Logan could ask for clarification, because he knew damn well HFH had nothing big planned just then, Cage hurried on. "What's your plan for tonight?"

In other words, the boss didn't want to talk about the big op.

What *was* his plan tonight? From anyone else, Logan would have considered the question prying, but Cage was a friend. He knew part of what had happened during the Trehern assignment, knew something of Sharilee's death. So Logan said simply, "I'm going to keep a sharp eye out. Nobody's going to hurt her, not on my watch."

He ended the call and stood for a moment in silence.

Then he crossed to a window that overlooked the dark street and looked down on nothing.

They were out there, waiting. He could sense them.

Chapter Three

Sam spent a dark, uneasy night in her bedroom. When she slept, she dreamed a dizzying melange of dark-rimmed hazel eyes and gunshots, of sex and fear. And each time she awoke tangled in her sheets and gasping for air, she heard hints of motion from the floor below, an occasional footstep or low murmur of one-sided conversation.

She wasn't sure which was worse—dreaming about Logan or knowing he was downstairs.

Finally, toward dawn she fell into a deep, dreamless sleep that was broken too early by the raucous ring of her bedside phone.

She grabbed the receiver before the second ring, brain mostly awake though her body was far behind. "This is Dr. Blackwell."

Only then did she realize that the sun shone between her heavy bedroom drapes. She'd overslept.

"Sam, it's Izzy. That horrible man is at it again, and I can't find Jimmy anywhere. You'll have to deal with it."

"Which man? Deal with what?" Spurred the rest of the way awake by the excitement in her neighbor's voice, Sam sat up in bed and smothered a curse when her hip howled in pain.

The bandaged cut burned like fire and the whole joint ached. She nearly whimpered for aspirin.

"Horace Mann," Izzy answered as though it should have been obvious. "He's fighting dogs in his barn, I'm sure of it. I went by there on my way to the transfer station and saw twenty trucks as sure as I'm breathing!"

A surge of adrenaline launched Sam the rest of the way out of her badly mussed bed. "Izzy, you're a goddess. I'll get over there right away and let you know how it goes."

She disconnected and immediately called Treece, but the dispatcher didn't know where Jimmy was, either. "Tell him I'm over at Mann's place," Sam said. "The bastard's pitting a dogfight."

She downed a strong dose of aspirin and pulled on clothes, hissing when her jeans pressed the bandage against her hip. If it wasn't for that pointed reminder, she might have convinced herself that the day before had been one of her restless dreams, that she hadn't been shot, that Logan Hart hadn't insisted on staying downstairs in her clinic all night, keeping watch.

But she *had* been shot, and he *had* stayed—a fact that became apparent the moment she limped down the stairs and into the waiting room. Though she'd expected him to be there, the foreknowledge didn't stop her stomach from doing a weird little shimmy number when she saw him fast asleep, stretched across some half-dozen padded chairs.

His face had relaxed in slumber, but it looked no less forbidding. Even in sleep, he was in control.

"Logan?" His name felt strange on her tongue, but after spending the night listening for his movements, a more formal address seemed equally strange. "Are you awake?" He clearly wasn't, but the sound of her voice was a breakfast call to the clinic patients, who set up a din of barks and yowls.

"Freeze!" Logan bolted to his feet in one smooth motion that had the shotgun up and aimed at the door between one of Sam's quick heartbeats and the next.

"Whoa, hey, no!" She jumped across the small space, grabbed for the gun and staggered when her injured leg folded.

He held the shotgun away and caught her with one strong arm, making her feel like a featherweight, though she was a curvy hundred and thirty pounds.

He scowled down at her, his face close enough that she could see the dark stubble on his jaw, the agitated pulse beneath the tanned skin of his throat. "What the hell do you think you're doing?"

Her hip burned from the bullet crease. Her body burned everywhere else from his touch, from the strength of the man against her and the knowledge that he was everything she had vowed not to want anymore. Because of it, she pushed away. "Waking you up, at least long enough to let you know that I'm leaving. Bloody Horace Mann is fighting dogs again."

When she headed for the door, he grabbed her arm. "You're not going anywhere. At least not until Jimmy and I find the shooters."

"Not an option." Annoyed by Logan's high-handed pronouncement and suffused with the urge to get to Mann's place *now,* to get away from Logan *now,* she pulled against his grip. When he didn't let go, she glared at him. "Listen. We've been trying to catch these bastards for nearly two years. Every time we get close, they change the location. A few months ago, one of the dogs got loose and savaged a little girl." She closed her eyes against the image and sucked in a breath, willing him to understand. "Izzy says they're fighting in Mann's barn, right now. I don't have time to debate this with you—Jimmy's incommunicado and I'm the only animal officer in town."

Some of the urgency must have penetrated, or else he realized there was no dissuading her, because he nodded. "Okay. Give me a minute."

"For what?"

"I'm coming with you." He held up a hand to cut off her automatic protest. "Jimmy called me around midnight. The rifle they found on the beach was wiped clean, but he figured we might get something off of trace or latent prints. He ran the rifle up to the state lab and is waiting for results."

Something in his expression stopped Sam's headlong rush out the door. She cocked her head. "What aren't you telling me?"

His jaw set, his distinctive eyes holding hers. "Viggo's usual muscle is all accounted for. We're not sure who he hired for the hit. It could be anyone."

She wasn't quite sure how that differed from where they'd been the night before, but the seriousness of his tone sent a shiver through her body. "So where does that leave us?"

He hefted the shotgun and gestured for her to get behind him. "That leaves you in my protection until Jimmy gets back from the state lab. I'd prefer to keep you safe in here, but I'm smart enough to know that's not happening. So I'm going with you to this dogfight. Got a problem with that?"

The rational, slightly scared part of her thought it sounded fine. But her heart rebelled, knowing it was safer for them to be far apart rather than risking the spontaneous combustion that was sure to follow if they spent too much time together.

And that included time spent in the small cab of her vet's truck.

"I don't know…" she began, but trailed off when she saw the implacable set to his jaw and the hard glint in his eye, one that reminded her quite strongly of her father when he was in Sheriff Bob mode. The image was oddly reassuring, so she nodded instead of arguing. "Okay. Come on, then."

They passed the ten-minute ride to the Mann place

in a tense, ready silence laced with things better left unspoken. Logan glared at the passing scenery and held
the shotgun in his lap until she turned down the narrow
road leading to the local transfer station.

Then he glanced at her. "What's the story on this guy?"

"Local thug," she answered, and concentrated on her
driving, on the urgency that beat in her chest. "I went
to school with one of his younger brothers. The whole
family was a little run-down, but the other kids did okay.
Two of them have good jobs in town, and one moved
out of state. Horace, though…he's rotten."

She'd love to bust one of Mann's dogfights. She was
sick of the local kids bringing her the torn up pit-bull
crosses and junkyard dogs Mann's buddies tossed in the
woods to die after their fights.

It was inhumane, and it was illegal. And she intended
to stop it.

"How smart is he?"

She slid a glance over at Logan. "Not that smart. I
doubt this is an ambush, or that he's working with the
shooter."

And what must it be like to even think that way? A
shiver crawled across her shoulders at how his mind
worked, at the experiences that must have shaped him
into the suspicious, on-edge man sitting beside her.

He seemed to accept her assurance, but part of her
wondered. So once she parked the truck in Mann's
driveway, she reached across Logan and grabbed her .38
out of the locked glove compartment. Just in case.

"Come on." She jumped out of the truck and tried to ignore the slow, creeping warmth that flared where her arm had brushed against his leg. "Look big and threatening."

"I can do that."

"I bet you can." Heart pounding with anticipation of a fight, she focused on the scene before her, though there was a sneaky warmth and a sense of safety from the man at her back.

Don't get used to it, girl. He's temporary.

Yeah, she acknowledged. Very temporary. Like on his way out of town.

Annoyed with the direction of her thoughts, she shoved them aside and strode toward the big red barn out behind Mann's one-story home. New this year, the barn had been built with the blood money she and Jimmy knew had come from a hundred illegal pit fights.

Now it housed them. It had to.

But Sam's heart sank as they rounded the corner of Horace's white-painted house and skirted the planted flower beds.

No cars. No barking or shouting.

"You sure about this?" Logan's voice sounded close behind her, closer than she'd expected. She jumped at the tone of it, and the sizzle of warmth that shot through her, reminding her once again that hormones were not to be trusted.

Especially not hers.

"I'm sure," she said, brazening out the sinking of her heart. "But we're too damn late."

As though in answer to her statement, the barn doors rolled opened. Horace Mann stood in the dark gap, eyes narrowed with a false smile. "Why, it's Dr. Blackwell. What a surprise. And who is this?" His eyes slid to Logan and she imagined they darkened a bit in worry.

"A trainee," she lied. "We got a call about dogs barking and a bunch of trucks parked back here. You wouldn't be pit fighting, would you?"

It galled her to play this game by the book, but her father had taught her that an illegal arrest was no arrest at all. Not that she could arrest the odious man, but Jimmy could—and would—the moment she had evidence.

"Me? Of course not." Mann shrugged and gestured deeper into the barn. "You're welcome to look around."

Which meant there was nothing to see. None of the bloodstained plywood the bettors used to make temporary fighting pits. No spiked collars or barbed ankle straps, no fur, no bloodstained floorboards or swept-up sand. And most important…

"Where are your dogs?" she asked after ten minutes of fruitless searching with both Logan and Horace on her heels.

"The dogs?" Mann shrugged. "At the groomer."

If the crossbred beasts Horace kept ostensibly to patrol his yard had ever seen the inside of Birdie White's grooming salon, Sam would eat kibble for a week. "Oh, really? And Birdie will confirm this?"

Mann wrinkled his nose. "Not Birdie. A friend of a friend."

"And when will they be returned?"

"Today, tomorrow." He shrugged. "Eventually."

In other words, whenever they healed up enough to reenter the pit. Frustration bubbled up inside Sam's chest, the familiar feeling of failure she experienced whenever she went toe-to-toe with Mann, who she often suspected was smarter than most of the locals thought.

Smarter than she liked. *Smart enough to get himself involved with Viggo Trehern?* a little voice asked in the back of her head.

No. Not that smart. But smart enough to cause trouble, nonetheless.

"Damn it," she said aloud, not caring that Horace smirked at her obvious defeat.

The bastards had been fighting dogs here not half an hour ago, she was sure of it. She could smell the blood and the violence. The locals—and some not-so-locals— had leaned over the bloody pit and shouted encouragement as the creatures had torn at each other, their natural instincts heightened with hormones, starvation and cruelty. Bets had been won and lost, the lookouts had done their jobs.

And in the end, the true losers were the dogs, who were likely dead or dying. Somewhere.

But until she could find a corpse, witnesses or evidence of a fight…she had nothing.

"Come on, let's go." She gestured toward Logan, who had yet to relax his bristling, protective stance. "There's nothing here."

Mann narrowed his eyes and his false smile edged toward something a little more sinister. "I could have told you that, Dr. Blackwell. And I'm getting tired of your harassment. I have half a mind to—"

With a movement so quick it caught her unawares, Logan spun and grabbed Mann by the shirtfront. "Obviously you have half a mind, so I'll speak slowly. Dr. Blackwell is doing her job. You and I both know you were fighting dogs here—the place stinks of blood."

Though his eyes bulged in their sockets, Horace managed a snort. "Ya can't testify to a smell and you've got nothing else on me."

"Not yet." Logan leaned close and glared. "But you keep this up and they will. When that happens, I'll be here to see that you're prosecuted...and convicted."

Logan's words weren't strictly a threat, but the punch of his tone, and the deadly stare that backed them up told Sam he wasn't kidding. The force and the barely restrained violence kicked heat into her stomach.

You don't like too-macho men, she told herself, though history said otherwise. Aloud, she said, "We're done here, Logan. Come on."

She didn't, as she had done so many times in the past, keep one eye behind her, in case Mann sicced one of the half-mad dogs on her or chased after her with his shotgun. She trusted that Logan had her back.

"And it doesn't matter worth a damn," she muttered to herself as she climbed into the truck, "because he's out of here the moment the deputies get back into town."

"What was that?"

She slammed her door. "Nothing. Come on, let's get out of here and see what Jimmy has on the rifle."

AT THE SHERIFF'S OFFICE a half hour later, Logan scowled at the report in his hand. "They didn't find a damn thing."

"Nothing useful, anyway." The sheriff raised an eyebrow. "Though they found their nothing damn quickly."

"I called in a few favors," Logan admitted, still frowning down at the report. When Samantha took it from him, he didn't protest. He'd seen everything there was to see.

Nothing. No prints. No trace evidence. No serial numbers. Nothing. Either these guys were professionals or they were very, very lucky.

Knowing Viggo as well as he did, Logan was betting on the former. Which left them no closer to identifying the shooters than they'd been the day before. And since Cage's big deal overseas meant that no other HFH operatives were readily available to make the trip to Black Horse Beach to back Logan up, there seemed to be only one good solution.

He glanced over at Samantha, knowing full well she wouldn't like it.

She caught the look. "What?"

"I think you should come to Boston with me. HFH can offer you protective custody until we've identified the shooter and Trehern's trial is over." He didn't mention that at the rate they were going, the trial could take months.

He half expected an explosion. He got a shrug. "No thanks." She handed the fruitless evidentiary report back to Jimmy, who seemed to be giving Logan's idea serious consideration. "I'll carry my .38, and the deputies can cruise past the clinic a few times per night, but I'm not leaving. My patients need me, and frankly, I'm not convinced that I'm in real danger."

Logan might have bought it if he hadn't seen her hand tremble. The sheriff noticed it as well, and reached out to touch Samantha's shoulder. "Sam, you should think about going. Jennifer can take care of the small animal stuff and refer the large animals to someone else. I'd hate for anything to happen to you."

She didn't move away from Jimmy's touch, which sent a sharp flash of annoyance through Logan's chest.

It was irritation, he told himself, not jealousy. He had no right to be jealous, no right to her at all, particularly not after what the sheriff had told him about her history. She deserved a steady man, one who wanted to stay in town.

A man like Sheriff Jimmy.

Logan turned away. "I have some calls to make. I'll be out in your truck when you're ready to run me back to my place."

Just because she wasn't for him didn't mean he wanted to watch her with someone else.

She joined him a few minutes later, sliding into the driver's seat with no explanation. "You ready?"

He nodded curtly as they set off down the road. He wished he didn't care who she spent time with, wished the idea of bringing her into the city for protective custody didn't sound so good. But the idea wouldn't leave his head.

He could set her up in one of Boston General's ultra-secure apartments. Better yet, she could stay in his rooms. During the day, he could do his damnedest to identify the shooter and ferret out what else Trehern planned for the short list of witnesses lined up to convict him. At night, he would sleep in an apartment nearby. Maybe they could share a meal. A movie. A conversation.

Maybe more.

The truck hit a bump, jolting him back to reality. What the hell was he thinking? Hadn't he just told himself she was far better off with Sheriff Jimmy than with him?

"You're scowling," she commented without looking at him. "What's wrong?"

What was wrong? Everything was wrong. He was stuck in Black Horse Beach protecting a woman who wanted things to run business as usual even though her life was in danger. Worse, he was attracted to her, and it seemed that the safest option was for them to enter protective custody.

Together.

So he frowned harder. "Nothing's wrong." She turned down a side road that hugged the rocky coast and he focused on the unfamiliar surroundings. "Where are we going?"

She stared straight ahead and concentrated on the twisty road. The view of ocean breaking on the rocks below was breathtaking. The view in the suddenly small-seeming cab no less compelling but far less simple.

After a moment, she glanced at him, then quickly looked away. "I have a stop to make. It'll only take a minute."

The last was said with a faint underlying challenge as she turned the truck between a pair of wide, sweeping granite pillars edged with curls of wrought iron.

A tasteful brass plaque read Bellamy Farms. Beneath the larger lettering ran a single boastful line: The home of the highest winning percentage ever in thoroughbred racing.

Sam parked as the silence stretched thin between them. "Come on, we'll need to walk from here. Bellamy is a tightly guarded operation."

Her words proved true moments later, when they were denied passage through a second ring of stone-and-iron fencing.

"Sorry, ma'am. I can't let you in." The fair-haired guard didn't bother to look at his paperwork or radio for confirmation.

Sam stopped and surprise flitted across her expressive face. "I was here two days ago, helping a little chestnut mare with her delivery. I just want to check on the foal. Surely you can give me five minutes."

Faint color washed up the guard's throat and his voice dropped from professional to young. "I'm sorry, Sam.

But Doc Sears is back from his conference, and he was furious when he found out you'd worked on the mare."

The faint tingle of suspicion in Logan's brain subsided. He could understand professional jealousy. In that, human and animal medicine weren't too far apart.

"Come on, Billy," Sam said quietly. "Five minutes, nothing more. I'll put in a good word for you with the sheriff the next time the deputy's exam comes up." She smiled, but Logan could see from the tightness around her eyes and mouth that she was ticked. And hurt.

It was odd how well he'd come to know her in such a short time.

The guard shook his head. "No can do, Sam. Honest. Doc Sears left strict instructions and Mr. Bellamy backed them up."

"Damn it! I'm good enough to spend six hours saving the life of a foal that was too big for its mother in the first place, but the moment Sears returns, I'm not even good enough to get in the front door?"

She cursed sharply enough to startle Logan, but when she turned away from the guard shack and stalked back toward the screened parking area where they'd left the vet-mobile, he thought he glimpsed tears.

"Samantha." He caught her arm. "Sam. Are you okay?"

"Fine." She glared at him through wet, angry eyes, and the flash in their depths told him she felt the sizzle of contact, too.

He dropped his hand and backed away. "Sorry."

"Yeah. Me too." She rubbed her arm where he had

touched it, then swung into the truck and cranked the starter so hard it whined. "Get in. We'll head back to the clinic."

They were silent for half a mile before she burst out, "Do you know how hard I've struggled to get work at that barn? The fees from being their backup vet alone would make a huge dent in the money I spend on the shelter." She banged the steering wheel and took a sharp corner a little too fast, sending gravel skidding off the road to the cliffs and water below. "That little mare would've died without me. Sure, Dr. High-and-Mighty Sears didn't expected her to pop so early, and he wouldn't have known the foal was butt-first, but damn it! I thought this was going to be my big break."

"Sorry," he said, though the word seemed inadequate.

She shot him a glare. "Oh, what do you care? You want me to up and leave town because of trouble *you* got me into. How is that fair?"

"It isn't," he agreed, knowing it wasn't him she was mad at, but glad to see her blowing off some steam. "But it's really for the best."

She shot daggers at him. "I knew renting the cottage to you was a bad idea the moment I laid eyes on you."

Logan reminded himself she had a right to be ticked. But her anger resonated with the edgy, spiky energy he felt at her nearness, at their situation. His own blood heated a notch. "Well, I'm sorry if my—"

"Logan!" she shouted. "The brakes don't work!" She

tromped the pedal and grabbed the steering wheel with both hands.

The truck didn't slow.

His stomach vised. The curve of Third Cliff came too fast. Too sharp. *"Look out!"*

Samantha screamed, spun the wheel and hit the brakes again, but the truck didn't slow, didn't change course.

In fact, it sped up, headed toward the drop-off, and the rocks and foamy salt water below.

"Hang on!" He jammed a hand to the roof of the cab and grabbed a fistful of her shirt, just as the truck crashed through the flimsy guardrail and flew into empty space.

Chapter Four

"Logan!" Sam's seat belt locked across her hips and shoulder. The truck lunged out into nothingness and seemed to hang there.

The high tide crashed against rocks thirty feet below. A gull screamed. Logan grabbed her arm.

And they fell.

The back of the truck slammed into the cliff face and the recoil shot them away, toward the deep water below the cliff.

"Hang on!" Logan's shout was nearly lost amid the crash of a second impact.

Hang on to what? Sam thought, panicked, as the world spun and flailed. Their seat belts locked them in place, but the tumbling fall jolted her from side to side. So she grabbed for the solidest thing nearby.

Him.

The front of the truck hit a boulder, or maybe the foot of the cliff, and the back of the vehicle dropped with a lurch. The cab flipped like a carnival ride and

Sam screamed as the truck fell backward into the water.

Upside down.

"It's deep here!" she yelled over the gurgle around them and the pounding of her heart in her ears. "The cliff divers don't touch bottom!"

Panic locked her throat as she fought her seat belt and jerked the door handle. Out! She needed to get out! Oh, God, they were sinking. The truck listed onto its side and slowly dropped toward darkness. Toward death.

She shoved at the door, but it wouldn't open. Claustrophobia clawed through her and panic narrowed her focus to a pinprick as the light faded from day to twilight-green. The air in the medical equipment compartments in the back buoyed the vehicle enough to flip it right side up, but not enough to keep it afloat.

They were sinking. "Get me out of here! *I don't want to die!*"

"Samantha." Strong fingers closed on hers. "Calm down."

She yanked away. "Calm down? How do you expect me to calm down? The door won't open! We're sinking. We're—" Her seat belt gave way at last and she tumbled across the small cab.

Logan's arms closed around her, holding her still, trapping her.

"Let me go. We've got to get out!" She thrashed and howled, her long-outgrown fear of small, dark spaces rearing up to overwhelm her senses. *"Let me go!"*

"Samantha! *Sam!* Settle down!" His shout cut into panic's fog and she turned her face to his. Sharp amber pierced the fear and she took a breath. He grabbed her upper arms and shook her. "You with me now? You ready to get the hell out of here?"

She nodded, unable to trust her voice. The truck lurched and shuddered. She whimpered, but held onto the feel of his hands on her arms.

"Okay, I need you to blow out a couple of good breaths, then suck one in and hold it, okay? We're going to roll down the windows and let the water in. When the pressure has equalized, we'll be able to open the door, okay?" When she didn't respond, he shook her again. "Okay?"

How could he be so calm? They were sinking! The sea bubbled in, cooling her legs where they tangled with his. But his eyes demanded an answer, so she nodded. "Okay."

"Good. Stay with me. We're going to take those breaths now."

And they did. Eyes locked, they exhaled twice then inhaled, and he cranked his window down.

Cold water gushed in, startling the breath out of her. *Breathe! She had to breathe!* But he grabbed her hand and ordered, "Take another breath and hold it, now!"

Then he reached across her and rolled down the other window.

Water roared into the cab, filling it. Cold wetness bit through her clothes and dragged at the fabric. Everything was suddenly darker, as though they'd already hit bottom, as though there was no way out.

Sam's vision grayed. Her lungs collapsed on themselves, her brain cried out for her to breathe. Breathe! She closed her eyes and fought the panic, fought the need to howl.

Then she felt his strong grip on her wrist, pulling her out and up.

Up.

She opened her eyes and saw light overhead, glorious sunlight reflected off the surface. It seemed close enough to touch, yet too far to reach. Then Logan was beside her, an arm around her waist, kicking them both up toward the air.

Suddenly anxious to get away from her truck, she scissored her legs and cursed the drag of her light pants. She kicked off her loafers and swam hard with Logan at her side.

They broke the surface together and gasped for air.

Before they could rejoice, a wave crested over the top of them, and the tidal surge picked them up and tossed them toward the rocky face of Third Cliff.

New panic bloomed in Sam's chest. The cliff divers warned of undertows and strange tidal eddies that could crush a swimmer against the rocks in half a minute. They had to get the hell out of there.

"Swim!" She struck out on a diagonal, aiming for a small spit of sand beyond the cliff outcropping, where the local thrill seekers dragged themselves after jumping off the cliff right beside the No Diving sign. "This way!"

Logan passed her in a half-dozen strokes, then reached back to help her. "Come on, I've got you!"

A heavy wave picked them up and flung them toward shore. They bodysurfed the last fifty feet until they felt sand beneath them. Firm, glorious sand.

Oh, God. Shaking uncontrollably, she touched the yielding grit and felt tears press. Exultation swept through her.

We're alive!

"We made it!" Sam struggled to her feet, shackled by her sodden clothing and unsteady legs. She grabbed Logan, or maybe he grabbed her, and they staggered out of the surf line together, gasping for air and talking incoherently over each other with a blend of adrenaline and frantic relief.

When they reached the dry, fluffy sand, Logan dropped to the ground and pulled Sam with him. She rolled onto her back, luxuriating in the feel of solid land beneath her and letting the realization that they were safe flow through her like a promise.

Then he leaned over her, brows furrowed in concern. "Are you hurt? Sam, are you okay?" He ran a hand down her side, checking for injuries. Flames engulfed her from his touch.

Without thinking, without questioning her motives or the wisdom of the action, she reached up, locked her arms behind his neck and drew him down for a kiss.

She meant the gesture to say, We're alive. *Thank you!* But what might have begun as a gesture morphed into passion at the first touch of her lips to his. Heat chased away the chill of terror, and joy lightened her limbs and heart.

This is what she'd missed, she thought instantly. The flash and the flame. Only this was much more than she'd had with the others.

Logan's body stiffened at the first touch and his hand fisted in the sodden cloth of her drawstring pants. He held still for one heartbeat. Another. Then, with a startled, reverent oath he rolled fully against her and aligned their bodies soft to hard, smoke to flame.

The power of it rocketed through her even as she opened her mouth to touch her tongue to his and found him waiting for her.

Demanding her.

Their mouths mated greedily, almost violently, yet his hand was gentle at her hip, soothing the place where her bandage was soaked with salt water, just as he'd kept her calm long enough to pull her from the sinking truck.

At the memory of sinking, of space closing in on her, Sam tangled her legs with his and pressed nearer still, until it seemed she could slide inside his skin and absorb the heat and power of him. Or maybe that was her heat, her power, the energy that they made together.

Whatever the source, she reveled in it, in the feeling of being *alive* as she traced her lips along his jaw and arched against the feel of his hand sliding up her ribs to cup her breast.

Then it all ended, as abruptly as it had begun.

Conscious of the change, of the quick stillness of his entire body, she stiffened and jerked her eyes open, fearing an outside attack. But his attention was focused entirely on her, the molten heat of his dark-rimmed amber eyes seeming to spear into her core and fan the blaze of their bodies.

Oh, God. Their bodies. What the heck was she doing?

Sanity returned with a wet thud, leaving them staring at each other, hearts pounding, wondering what they had just done and what it might mean.

Or not mean.

"Um…" She swallowed hard and forced her voice steadier than that pitiful quaver. "Thanks for saving my life."

His expression darkened and he shifted away from her, so their bodies were no longer aligned in intimate proximity. As though that wasn't enough separation, he levered himself to his hands and knees, then rested back on his haunches. Beneath the wet material of his jeans and dark T-shirt, his body looked poised for fight, for flight, for just about damn near anything.

"Don't thank me." He gained his feet in a smooth, tightly coiled move, then reached a hand down to help her up. "If it wasn't for me you wouldn't have been in danger in the first place."

Sam's spinning brain refused to comprehend, but then the memory came. She'd hit the brakes and nothing had happened. Spun the wheel but there had been no response. She clenched her fists. "What? What are you saying?"

He blew out a frustrated breath and tugged her up the beach, away from the water and the place where her van had sunk. "Don't you get it? Your truck was sabotaged!"

Sabotage. The three syllables made no sense, as though he'd spoken in a foreign language. She shook her head and followed him along the beach, to the place where a sandy trail led between two rocky walls and climbed to the road above.

Impossible, she thought. This was Black Horse Beach. Sabotage was unthinkable.

Or at least it had been, until Logan came to town.

Sam slammed to a halt. "Why sabotage my truck? Why not yours? If you're the one they're after…"

He turned back, expression unreadable, though there was banked heat in the tightness of his jaw and the flare of his nostrils. "I told you. That's how Trehern works. He wants to get at me, so he'll get to the people I care about first."

"But you hardly know me!"

The sudden gleam in his eyes reminded her that they knew each other a whole lot better than they had minutes earlier, but instead of remarking on it, he growled, "That won't matter to Viggo. He knows the best way to get at me is through a woman."

The flat venom in his pronouncement was as much a surprise as the unexpected flare of jealousy that caught

Sam square in the chest. She bit back the sharp question and turned away to buy a moment to recover.

A glint high up on the cliff caught her attention.

Logan saw it in the same moment. "Down!" He pushed her to the sand, behind a jagged outcropping of rock, and covered her with his body.

Sam tensed for the shot, for the burn of another splinter in her hip, or worse, to feel his body jerk against hers. They were barely covered by the rock, and the open sand of the canyon stretched beyond them in either direction. They were sitting ducks, and that was no poacher up there.

But there was no shot.

After a long moment, Sam risked a peek over Logan's shoulder.

He hissed, "Stay down," but it didn't sound like he meant it. His voice reflected her confusion and his body relaxed its protective embrace.

"Is he gone?"

Before Logan could answer, approaching footsteps told the story. Stones rattled at the entrance to the canyon, breaking free beneath the force of a man's measured tread.

Logan cursed and flattened her to the sand, covering her completely with his body for protection as dire foreknowledge thundered through her like fear.

They should have run when they had the chance, should have—

"Am I interrupting something?" The voice held no amusement.

Relief sizzled through Sam when she recognized Jimmy's tones, followed quickly by fear. "Jimmy, get down! There's someone at the top of the cliff!"

But Logan levered off her and offered a hand. "No, he'll be gone by now. Viggo's men don't generally mess with cops. At least not when they're in uniform."

Sam might have wondered at the complex layer of emotion she detected in his voice, but Jimmy didn't give her the chance. The moment she was on her feet, he grabbed her.

"Are you okay?" When she didn't answer right away, he shook her gently. "Sam, are you hurt? Darryn Franks's boy was on Second Cliff. He saw the truck go over and called it in…"

Sam heard the ragged concern in her friend's voice. She tore her attention away from Logan's tense, stiff-legged stance and the jangling buzz of his body against hers, and focused on Jimmy. His eyes held worry and fear. Caring and concern.

For her.

The sight of it broke through the numb, disbelieving barriers that had buffered her from the accident, from the belief that something so awful, so terrifying had happened to her. She started to shake, and couldn't stop. Tears gathered at the corners of her eyes.

"Sam? Are you hurt?" Jimmy stepped closer even as Logan strode down the beach, staring up at the cliff.

"N-no." She shook her head and tried to pull it together, tried to hold on to the strength her father had taught her. But toughness was a ragged cloak around her shoulders that let through drafts of fear. "Not hurt. But the truck—"

The truck was in the ocean, along with all her equipment. She imagined it tilted on the rocky sea floor amid the dark green water, with the windows rolled down.

What would have happened to her if Logan hadn't been there to calm her? To roll down the windows and let the pressure equalize?

In her mind, her own face pressed against the rolled up driver's side window and she moaned.

"You're hurt." Jimmy gathered her under his arm, though his embrace didn't even begin to push back the ice gathered around her heart. "I'm taking you to the hospital."

"No." She resisted when he tried to lead her up the beach, away from Logan. "There was someone up on the cliff." She pointed above, to where they'd seen the glint.

The skyline was empty now, but that didn't mean the person was gone. He could be waiting. The moment she and Jimmy left—

Boom. Logan would be unprotected.

"I'm calling in the state cops," Jimmy answered without really answering. "We'll wait for them. If this really is Viggo Trehern…" He shook his head. "I can't risk the safety of the townspeople." But his sideways blue-eyed glance told Sam the decision was as much for her as for anyone.

"No." Anxiety pounded through her, hot and hard,

though she wasn't totally sure of its source. "We can't wait. We need to get up there right away."

And they needed to take Logan with them. Halfway down the beach, he was in full view of all three cliffs, which stood stony sentinel over the deep inlet waters. When he turned out toward the sea and spread his arms wide, Sam suddenly understood what he was doing.

He was drawing fire. Or trying to.

"Logan, get back here!" she shouted, not caring that her voice shrilled on his name. Jimmy's iron grip held her from going after him, but Logan turned at her shout, shook his head, and retraced his steps across the sand.

His expression was thunderously cold. He passed her without a word, as though they hadn't shared a moment of pure, intense connection in the truck, as though they hadn't tried to crawl inside each other's skins on the beach, hadn't shared a blazing kiss that should have been more, couldn't have been less.

"Logan?" she said quietly, and the single word brought him up short.

He turned back, but didn't look at her. His hunter's stare was directed at the sheriff. "I need you to drive us back to the clinic. You can call reinforcements from there."

"Wait." Sam would have stepped toward him, but his closed expression held her off as surely as Jimmy's iron grip. "What are you going to do?"

His eyes flickered briefly to her, then away. "I'm going to get my truck and make two stops. Then I'm picking you up and we're heading into the city. You're not safe here. Your brakes were tampered with!"

Her instinctive denial that she didn't want to leave Black Horse Beach, didn't want to go into protective custody, was blunted by the shakes and the image of her own face inside a blue-green shrouded truck. Her brakes had been fine leaving the sheriff's office. Or had they? It didn't make any sense to think someone at Bellamy Farm had tried to hurt her. Then again, none of it made sense.

Jimmy let go of her arm and stepped forward. "I'll need you to stay in town until the others arrive. They'll have questions for you."

Logan's stare measured the other man. "You don't want me to do that."

"You're right, I don't. But it's procedure." And like Sam, Jimmy had learned his guts and his rules from Sheriff Bob. And to Sam's father, procedure was God.

"Very well then." Logan inclined his head and Sam felt a spurt of relief that they wouldn't be leaving immediately, after all.

Though part of her wanted to run screaming toward the haven deep inside Boston, where Logan had promised they could keep her safe, an equally strong part of her wanted to run screaming in the other direction. Because while her body might be safer in the city under Logan's protection, she knew with a certainty born of the passion they'd shared on the shoreline that her heart was safer far, far away from him.

She'd chosen unwisely before, and each goodbye had taken a piece of her soul.

Something told her this goodbye would take the rest of it.

"Sam? You coming?" Jimmy's question roused her and she was surprised to realize Logan was already gone. Angry footsteps gouged in the sand showed where he'd stalked through the narrow canyon, up toward the road where Jimmy must have parked.

Logan's absence relaxed her at the same time that it worried her. He'd kept her safe twice now, and she was tempted to cling.

Because of it, she turned to Jimmy. "Is this the only way?"

"You think I like it?" His sudden ferocity startled her, as did the fire in his eyes when he rounded on her and grabbed her arms. "You think I like knowing that I'm not good enough to protect you? That I'm not good enough to—" He broke off with an oath and released her arms. "Come on. If we don't hurry, he'll leave without us."

"Jimmy." Sam touched his arm and felt him stiffen. "It's not about being good enough. It's about…" She trailed off, not sure what it was about anymore.

"Yeah, I know." Surprisingly, he smiled and took her hand. "It we were meant to be, we would've figured it out a long time ago, wouldn't we?"

"I think so." She looked up into his dear face, seeing the boy inside the man. A band tightened around her heart and her stomach clenched on a beat of sadness for something that had never come to pass. She took a breath and wished things had been different, wished *she* had been different. "So I guess that means we're not meant to be."

Why did it feel like they were breaking up? They'd never been together, never kissed as more than friends.

But he'd been her safety net. Her fallback. The man she knew she could turn to if it came to it.

And that, Sam realized with a start, hadn't been fair to either of them.

From the glint in the sheriff's eye, he knew it, too.

"Well." She blew out a breath and realized that though the band around her heart had loosened, sadness lay heavy in her soul. "I guess this conversation has been too long in coming."

"Maybe we needed to get around to it in our own time," Jimmy said mildly, still holding her hand. But his attention was fixed on the cliffs above, and the deeply gouged footprints in the sand. "Though I wish we'd gotten here for a different reason."

When he returned his gaze to her, his eyes left no question as to his meaning. He wished she weren't in danger, wished Logan Hart had never entered their unsteady equation.

"I know what you mean." Sam glanced toward the path, toward the road and Jimmy's car, where Logan awaited them. But did she really wish he'd never come to Black Horse? Did she really wish they'd never met?

Jimmy tightened his fingers on hers. "Be careful, Sam. Please be careful."

She nodded. "I will. I promise."

But she didn't think either of them was talking about the shooter.

And she wasn't sure she could keep her promise.

THE SHERIFF INSISTED on stopping atop the cliff to look around. Logan would have rather gone back to the clinic and snagged his own truck. He wanted Samantha away from this. Now. Before she ended up like Sharilee.

In his mind, the image of a sexy vet with luminous eyes tangled with the memory of a darker, harder woman he'd thought a hooker.

Because of the guilt, and his impotent rage at the dangerous situation, he glared out the window of the sheriff's car at the passing beach plums and ground his teeth. When they reached the scenic-view pulloff at the top of Third Cliff, he was the first one out of the car.

He froze at the sight of the broken, twisted guardrail and a few uprooted beach plums where Sam's truck had gone through.

"It seems like there should be more," she said, limping up beside him, both arms wrapped around her torso.

"Yeah," he said gruffly, "skid marks."

His gut twisted like the crumpled metal railing as he remembered the plunge downward, the horrible sensation of sinking. He hated small, enclosed places and the thought of drowning, but he'd held it together and gotten them out of there.

Barely.

His hand itched to reach for her, but he forced himself to remain still. Their kiss had been a living fantasy, their seeming connection an artifact of the situation, of the stress and the fear. She wouldn't like the man he was.

Hell, *he* didn't like the man he was—or at least what he could recognize of himself. Before he'd joined HFH, he'd been a debonair transplant surgeon on a quick rise to the top of the Boston General hierarchy. But a case involving switched transplant organs had introduced him to HFH and their investigative teams, and he'd been immediately fascinated. Not long after, he'd joined HFH as an investigator, looking for danger, for excitement, for the opportunity to make a larger difference.

These days, he thought of the transplant department with a hint of wistfulness.

Sam would have liked the man he had been back then. He'd been considerate. Classy. He'd come home to his bachelor's apartment every night except when he was in surgery. He'd dated, sometimes seriously, never quite moving beyond an occasional sleepover and a regretful parting some weeks or months later. He'd wanted a family eventually, and figured he had time yet to find his match. Back then, he'd known who he was and where he was going.

That was the sort of man Sam needed. Not some burned out whatever he was, who woke up in a cold sweat some nights and didn't even go to sleep others. A man who'd stood by, helpless, and seen a woman executed. A man who, like Nancy's missing husband, might go off on assignment one day and never come home.

"Logan? Are you okay?" Sam touched his arm, recalling him from memory. He looked over and saw the sheriff standing at the edge of the cliff, shaking his head at the place they'd driven off.

Sam made no move to walk over to the gap. Neither did Logan. He had no wish to look over and relive that horrible moment when he'd realized the brakes had failed, that they were going over. Even now, the image and the possibilities sent ice through his soul.

The sheriff turned away from the water, from the place where Sam's truck rested on the ocean floor. "There's not much to see."

"I'm not surprised." Logan shoved his hands in his pockets as a reminder not to reach for the woman beside him, to comfort her, or maybe to comfort himself. "Trehern uses only the best. They're not sloppy."

Yet they'd failed to neutralize their targets twice. The contradiction worried Logan, though he was grateful for the failures.

"We'll let the state-lab boys look at the area." Jimmy strode back to his vehicle. "Maybe they'll get something off the tire tracks. And we'll see about salvaging the truck."

All three of them glanced to the gap where guardrail had given way to cliff. Logan pictured the rocks and the riptides, and knew it would be difficult to recover the truck. He shrugged. "That'll only prove what we already know. The brake lines were cut."

Sam shivered very slightly and Jimmy shot him a glare, but said only, "Come on. Let's head back to the clinic. I believe you wanted to retrieve your truck."

But once the tense, silent drive was accomplished and Logan sat alone in his vehicle, something stopped him from turning the key and driving to the cottage, where he planned to pack fast and get the hell out.

It wasn't fear for Sam, who would be well guarded by Jimmy—too well guarded, in Logan's opinion, though he had no right to the burst of jealousy. And it wasn't fear of what might await him at the cottage, although he intended to check everything out thoroughly before opening the front door, as Viggo Jr. had a fondness for plastique and gruesome gestures.

No, it was something more complicated than fear, though that was part of it. This emotion swelled his chest and battered his brain like nerves, but also warmed his gut like pleasure.

"To hell with it." Shoving aside introspection as being silly and unhelpful, he twisted the key. The truck roared to well-tuned life at the same moment his personal cell phone rang inside the glove box.

Logan popped the compartment open and retrieved the phone, new anxiety tightening his gut. Only Cage and his family had the number.

"Hello?"

He heard weeping—broken, wrenching sobs that tore straight to his heart and stopped it dead.

His fingers tightened on the phone and dread clutched his gut. "Nancy? Nance, what's wrong?"

"They found Stephen."

Chapter Five

It took a moment for Logan's brain to shift from thoughts of Samantha and Trehern to thoughts of his sister and her missing husband. Once they did, her words hit him with a nearly physical blow.

Nancy and Stephen had been married less than two years. He'd been missing for three months of that time. Now Nancy's sobs told the story.

"Is he..." dead? But Logan couldn't finish the question. He was too aware what Stephen's disappearance had done to his sister, too aware of what his death might do to her normally strong will.

"He's alive!" At her shout, laughter mixed with the tears in her voice, incredulous, joyous laughter that left Logan far behind. His heart scrambled to catch up, to rejoice.

"What? Where?" Even as he asked, even as he tried to share his sister's relief, Logan was conscious of a sense of urgency, conscious of Samantha's face peering through the wide front window of the clinic, and doubly aware of the sheriff standing behind her.

Too close.

"Logan? Did you hear me?"

"Yes, of course." He repeated the important information back. "The Tehruvian government has him in custody." Then the full import of her words registered and he focused sharply. "Tehru? Damn, Nancy, why didn't you tell me that's where he was?"

Once host to HFH relief efforts ranging from medical help for victims of earthquakes and mud slides to politically neutral first-aid camps during a viciously bloody civil war, Tehru was now on the interdict list for many foreign-aid agencies. The fighting had gotten too sharp, the factions too willing to capture foreigners for ransom.

So what had an HFH infectious-disease guy been doing there?

"I didn't know he was in Tehru." A quiver behind the words betrayed fear, or maybe anger. "He couldn't tell me where he was going. He was arrested for…I'm not even sure for what, but they're asking for a ransom. That's good news, they tell me. The ransom is good news. It means he's probably alive." Her voice broke on the last word.

Logan let out a breath and felt his chest ache with contradictory emotions—joy that Stephen was alive, fear that he was being held in a place like Tehru. "God, I'm sorry I'm not there."

But he couldn't go to Nancy and risk Viggo's men following. He couldn't leave Samantha here, not when her danger was his fault. And he couldn't miss the Trehern trial, which resumed in three days. But family was family, so he said, "What can I do?"

Something in his voice must have alerted her, or else her big-sister radar was activated, because her voice changed. "Logan, is something wrong? What's going on?"

"Nothing you need to worry about," he said flatly, wishing it weren't a lie. But his eighteen months undercover with Trehern had taken a toll on Nancy and their parents, and he wasn't about to drag them back to that place again. Especially considering the news about Stephen. "Do you want me to make a few calls?"

He'd earned some federal-sized markers in the aftermath of the Trehern sting. When the conviction went through, he'd have even more.

If the conviction went through. If Trehern didn't manage to kill or compromise the small pool of witnesses.

"I want you to pray for him," said Nancy, who had held on to more of their parents' faith than Logan had managed. "And I want you to keep yourself safe."

"Will do." They left the rest unspoken, but Nancy, the wife of an operative herself, knew the score. Logan trusted that she'd keep the knowledge from their parents, and tuck her worry for him beside that for her husband. The knowledge gave him an obscure sense of comfort, even though watching her over the past three months had helped to solidify his determination to avoid a serious relationship.

He couldn't ask another woman he cared about to live through such horror.

"I'll call when I have more news. Cage said he'd let me know the moment they've made a decision." Though they both knew what the decision would be. The U.S. government—and by extension HFH—didn't negotiate with terrorists. It would be a rescue attempt or nothing.

"I'll keep the phone with me." Logan could promise her that much but nothing more, not right then. But when she murmured goodbye, he quickly said, "Nance?"

A pause, then a tentative, curious, "What?"

"I'm sorry Stephen got you into this." Logan took a breath and wondered whether he was expressing sympathy for Stephen's abduction or his own choices. But guilt rang hollow with the knowledge that if he hadn't brought Stephen home with him after an early training op, Nancy wouldn't be in this situation now. "I'm sorry I didn't introduce you to a businessman, or a store owner or something."

This time the pause was longer before she said, "If he was either of those things, he wouldn't be the man I fell in love with, would he?"

The quiet, rational question stumped Logan for a moment. "You mean you don't wish he'd stayed home with you?"

She gave a watery laugh. "I'd be lying if I said that. And I'd be lying if I told you I don't lie awake some nights, cursing him for getting on that plane, cursing him for wanting to be a hero. But you know what? That doesn't mean I wish he was someone else." She paused and her voice changed. "Who is she?"

"There's nobody," he said quickly, even as his eyes were drawn once again to the clinic window, which was empty now. "I don't get serious about women. You know that."

"I know that's what you tell me." Nancy's voice softened, reminding him of the times she'd soothed him through childhood pains and chivied him through a resentful adolescence, well into her mother-hen role though she was a scant two years older than him.

"It's the truth."

"If you say so. But if it helps, the answer is no. I don't wish Stephen was something else. He is who he is." She stressed the present tense, as though needing to convince herself he was still alive. "And I wouldn't change him for the world because I love him just like I love you."

It humbled him that even at the lowest point of her life, or maybe the highest, he wasn't quite sure which yet, Nancy still tried to comfort him.

"Same here, Nance." He clicked the phone shut with a strange mix of guilt and confusion. Guilt that he couldn't race to the military base where Nancy currently lived in protective custody, and sit with her while she waited for news—or better yet, fly to Tehru and make something happen. Confusion from her words, and from a fleeting wish that he had someone to love him as deeply as his sister loved her husband.

But pretty words aside, he didn't completely believe

her. No woman in her right mind would willingly choose to love a man who might leave for work one day and never return.

He thought of Stephen. Of Sharilee. Of himself and the man he'd become in Trehern's world.

Gritting his teeth, he slammed the truck in reverse and accelerated out of the clinic driveway, away from the empty window, away from Samantha.

But the hell of it was he knew he'd be back—to protect her, if nothing else.

SAM FORCED HERSELF not to watch him drive away. Forced herself not to wonder who he'd been talking to on the phone, what they might have told him. It could have been a break in the case.

It could have been a woman. Perhaps even the one who'd put those shadows in the back of his eyes and the rage in his soul. But no, he said she'd died, hadn't he?

She tried to remember his exact words on the beach, when he'd told her how Trehern had used a woman to punish him. And though she couldn't remember the words, she could call back the sound of his voice and the feel of his body against hers.

"He's not Black Horse Beach material." For half a second, Sam thought the words were hers, playing in her head. Then her partner, Jennifer, touched her shoulder. "He won't stay."

"Of course he won't," Sam answered, automatically on the defensive. "Who asked him to?"

Jen tilted her head so her straight blond hair fell free. Her clear blue eyes, clouded with worry, silently reminded Sam how long they'd been friends. What they'd been through together.

Friends through vet school, the two had drifted apart after Jen's marriage to a young, rising politician and Sam's to Travis. When Jen's marriage had crashed and burned, she had come back to Black Horse and found Sam divorced and on the verge of opening the clinic with too little money. The serendipity had seemed like a lucky break for both of them.

It still did. Five years later, Sam had been through two more relationships and Jen none. Some days it seemed like she was waiting for something.

Or someone.

"I'm not trying to pry or tell you what to do." A rueful smile touched Jen's lips. "God knows it's never worked before. But you've said it yourself—no more temporary guys."

Actually, Sam's vow had been more along the lines of *no more drop-dead sexy, brooding temporary guys.*

All of which hit too close to home.

Chastened, Sam let her shoulders drop. "I'm sorry. It's been a long day." And it wasn't over yet. As soon as Logan was done with his preparations, they would leave for Boston.

She hated the city.

No, that wasn't entirely true. She enjoyed the city. But she hated that it drew so many good people away from the small towns, and sent so many tourists in return. Tourists who bought flea-market puppies in June and left them behind in late August when they disappeared back to their city lives. Tourists who crowded around Horace Mann's fighting pits and bet on the dogs.

But in fairness, it wasn't the city's fault the people acted that way.

Sam crossed her arms and frowned as she stared out the wide window, trying to avoid Jennifer's knowing eyes and the unfinished conversation that hung between them. "Fine. I'm in trouble. Are you happy now?"

Both of them knew she wasn't talking about the danger, though there was that, too.

"Just be careful, Sam. Please be careful. Of him. Of the…situation." Jen shrugged helplessly. "I don't want to see you hurt."

If the words seemed inadequate, the feeling behind them was anything but. The emotion hung heavy in the air until Jimmy barged in carrying a pizza box.

"You ladies hungry? My dad brought some over for us from the restaurant."

His voice was startlingly male in the clinic waiting room, and both women jumped. Sam because she was on edge from…well, from everything. And Jen because…

Just because.

"Sure." Sam took a slice to be polite and chewed it in small bites, deliberately not looking at the clinic doorway, where her two small suitcases awaited Logan's return. She tried not to think about the danger and failed, tried not to think about being near Logan and failed.

"Thanks." Jen took a slice, but didn't bite in as she carefully looked anywhere but directly at the sheriff.

The tension in the room grew. The silence thickened.

Suddenly, a deep-throated growl erupted from the recovery room. Then a furious fusillade of barks.

"What the—?" Sam was on her feet, halfway across the waiting room before Jimmy grabbed her.

"Wait! Let me go first."

God, she thought, *was someone in the clinic?*

Maverick's barking escalated to near frenzied. The sheriff stepped into the recovery room and fanned it with his weapon. Then he jerked his head for Sam to enter. "It's clear."

But what was wrong?

Maverick stood in his cage, plastered leg stuck out at an odd angle, every hair on end, barking as though the very hounds of hell had come to get him. The sight was enough to give her the shivers.

Aware of Jimmy and Jen behind her, Sam crouched by the cage but didn't reach a hand through. "Settle down, fella. Nothing's wrong. Nobody's going to hurt—"

An explosion split the air. The floor rocked beneath her.

And Maverick whined in fear.

Sam shot to her feet, heart pounding. "What the hell was that?"

But she didn't need to ask. Shock and sick certainty paralyzed her, made her want to scream a denial.

There was only one structure in the direction of the explosion.

Her rental cottage.

LOGAN WAS HALF-CONSCIOUS, pinned beneath a heavy oak countertop, but he heard them coming. Jimmy's radio squawked at his hip as he ran into the cottage. Sam remained quiet, but even so, Logan knew she was there.

He sensed her.

He would have warned her off, but it was no use. He didn't think she'd listen to him, and the bastard who'd rigged the explosive was long gone.

But he'd left a present.

"Sonofabitch booby-trapped the refrigerator," Logan grated when Sam and the sheriff hurried into the kitchen.

Sam dropped to her knees beside him with a cry of distress and touched his wrist for his pulse. "What happened? How badly are you hurt?"

"I was behind the door." At least he'd been smart enough to instinctively open the fridge away from himself. If he'd been standing directly in front of it, reaching for a soda…

Boom.

"Help me get this off of him." Jimmy grabbed one end of the oak countertop and gestured for Sam to get the other. It couldn't weigh more than a couple, three hundred pounds, but Logan had no leverage. No power.

He tried to be grateful when Samantha lifted the slab

with relative ease and slid it aside, but it galled the tough-guy core of him he'd developed by necessity in Trehern's employ. Samantha shouldn't rescue him, it should be the other way around, like it had been in the sinking truck.

And wouldn't Nancy be disappointed in him to hear that?

Unaccountably ashamed, Logan let Sam haul him to his feet once she'd assured herself there were no broken bones. "Thanks."

The word came out gruffly, but at least he'd made the gesture. A sick twist in his stomach told him his preoccupation with Sam's strength was nothing more than avoidance of the fact that he'd been a nanosecond from death by refrigerator bomb.

He shoved his hands in his pockets, joined Jimmy beside the now-gutted refrigerator and surveyed the damage. The old heavy-duty white-and-chrome appliance still sat in the nook between counter and stove, but all resemblance to a normal kitchen ended there. Focused by the thick metal walls of the refrigerator, the blast had had only one exit—out through the open door, directly toward an unwary snacker.

The inner walls of the fridge were blackened and melted, and the door had been blown across the room. Cabinet doors hung half-off, their meager bachelor-friendly contents forced to the back of the shelves or onto the floor.

"Luckily I don't cook much, or this would've been

a real mess." Logan's weak joke fell like lead. Sam pressed the back of her hand to her mouth and her eyes filled. He took a step toward her. "I'm sorry. I'm so sorry that I came here, that I brought this here—"

She backed away, shaking her head. But when she spoke, her voice was firm, her eyes sharp with anger through the moisture. "Don't. Apologize." She glanced around the devastated kitchen, then advanced on him. "You didn't ask for this. Neither of us did."

But in a way he had, just as Stephen had asked for trouble by following orders into Tehru. At the thought, the last of the adrenaline faded away, leaving him with sore reminders of the past two days, bruises that sang and pulsed.

"I don't suppose you saw anything?" Jimmy asked. He poked through the wreckage of the once-nice kitchen table Logan had broken on impact.

"Nothing." When the world fuzzed ever so slightly and he had to raise his voice above the tinny ring in his ears, Logan braced his feet a little wider and scowled. "Viggo's son likes plastique, though."

"Smells like ANFO to me." The sheriff crouched down to the floor but didn't touch. "Homemade stuff. We'll let the state boys have at it. They should be here any time now. When I radioed them about the explosion they were nearly at the town line."

All three fell silent, instinctively listening for approaching sirens.

They heard a dog barking, fast, hard and loud.

"That's Maverick!" Samantha's face reflected shock, then horror, and she gasped, "*Jennifer!*"

The sheriff bolted from the cottage. When Sam tried to follow, Logan grabbed her arm. "Wait! Who's Jennifer?"

She turned stricken eyes on him. "My best friend. We left her in the clinic."

And Trehern's men were on the loose, looking for a lady vet. Oh, hell.

"Come on!" Logan ran for the door, not letting go of her arm. His hand slid down and their fingers linked and held.

They ran up the sandy street together, spurred on by the dog's frenzied barks and the wail of approaching sirens. The staties arrived just as Logan and Sam pelted up the clinic steps and burst through the waiting room door.

A furry yellow body hurtled through the air toward them, echoing with blood-curdling growls. Logan lurched back and grabbed for the weapon he'd left behind in the cottage.

Sam stepped forward, deftly grabbed the dog by the loose skin at the scruff of its neck, and pinned it to the wooden floor, being careful of the beast's snapping teeth and plastered leg. She gestured over to the sign-in desk with her chin. "Grab me that nylon muzzle. We'll need to restrain him." She raised her voice. "Jennifer? Jen, are you okay?"

Jimmy's quiet voice answered from the recovery room. "She's in here."

Samantha moaned low, clearly fearing the worst, and

with good reason. Logan handed her the nylon contraption and let his hand linger on her shoulder. When the still-growling yellow dog was restrained, she let it up and kept a firm grip on its collar.

Behind them, a half-dozen men and women in state uniforms mounted the steps, but Logan paid them little heed as he and Sam crossed the waiting area to the recovery room.

There, they found Jimmy crouched down beside a pretty blond woman about Sam's age, about Sam's height and weight.

She was alive. Weeping. Seemingly in one piece.

"Jen!" The name drove out of Sam on a breath. She flung the yellow dog's leash at Logan and dropped to her knees, nearly shoving the sheriff aside. "What happened? Are you okay?"

"Maverick saved me." The woman's eyes darted to the yellow dog who stood, stiff legged and bristling, in the corner beside Logan. "He started barking again, so I came in here to talk to him. Then I heard something in the back room. A footstep." Her words came quick and breathy, from the shock. "I called for you and Jimmy, but you didn't answer. I got scared and didn't know what to do..." She trailed off and buried her face against Samantha.

"So you let Maverick out." Sam stroked her friend's hair. "That was a smart answer." She glanced over at Logan and he read pain in her eyes, guilt, and the fear of what might have happened if Jennifer had been a little slower, if the dog had been a little less alert.

Logan's mind showed him the body of Sharilee Winters, sprawled in indelicate disarray on the floor of Viggo's office.

Only the body didn't wear Sharilee's slightly hard, slightly used face.

Instead he saw Sam.

Acid churned in Logan's stomach. How had things gotten this bad this fast?

Because Viggo was a professional, and so were the men who worked for him. The hit had been unsuccessful so far, but more from blind luck than anything.

They couldn't count on that any longer.

As the staties eased into the room and began their investigation, Logan reached a hand down to Samantha. "It's time to go."

She glanced up at him, eyes dark with emotion, arms still wrapped around her friend. "You're right."

He wasn't surprised by her easy agreement. Like him, a threat to someone she cared about was a far more effective incentive than a threat to her own body, God help him.

But what did surprise him was the fire in her eyes when she took his hand and rose gracefully to her feet. "It's time for us to nail these bastards to the wall."

The declaration brought a nasty, sick sinking sensation to his stomach, as did her expression, which had probably come straight from the local legend known as Sheriff Bob.

The sheriff's daughter was going to war.

And how the hell was Logan going to keep her safe if she wanted to help investigate? He couldn't, that was how.

Because of it, and because of the need that tightened his belly at the feel of her hand in his, he dropped the contact and turned away. "Come on, then. We can be in Boston in three hours."

Then it would be time to set some ground rules.

He knew full well she wouldn't like the rules one bit, but they might keep her alive long enough for him to find Viggo's hired thugs and make sure they never bothered anyone ever again.

Especially her.

Chapter Six

Sam drove because Logan looked like hell. He refused to see a doctor, claiming it was nothing, but she knew a mild concussion when she saw one. And besides, his truck was easy enough to drive. It was virtually identical to hers, with the addition of a back seat and a single forward-swinging door.

Except hers had contained all of her large-animal equipment. And it was at the bottom of the ocean.

The state authorities said they'd salvage the vehicle as evidence, but all of her stuff was toast. Gone. A write-off.

Not unlike her rental cottage. The kitchen could be fixed, but insurance would only cover so much. She'd barely budgeted enough to manage the shelter through the slow winter season, and now this? She'd even had to leave Jen in charge of the small-animal work and turned the large-animal customers away.

Three days ago, she'd been looking to expand her clientele by taking on Bellamy Farms. Now she might as well roll over and declare bankruptcy.

"Insurance should cover most of it."

She turned a startled glance over to the passenger's side of the wide bench seat. Logan had been silent since they'd passed the Black Horse town line and hit the highway, headed for Boston. An hour into the trip, she was surprised to see his hazel eyes open and clear. "I thought you were asleep. And how did you know I was thinking about the damages?"

"Just a hunch. You have that pinched look people get when they're worried about money."

"Pinched. Gee, thanks." Irritation spiked. What did he know about it? He was an M.D., and probably collected hazardous duty pay on top of it. Though he dressed casually, his clothes were all of the highest quality, and where her truck had—used to have—vinyl and plastic, his boasted chrome and leather.

Then she sighed and dialed it down, knowing that though the money would be a real concern when this was all over and she returned to her life in Black Horse, that wasn't the real issue now, wasn't what really had her tense and on edge.

"You'll be safe in the city," he said, his voice gruff.

She stared fiercely through the windshield, unwilling to look over at him, to be caught once again in his eyes. "What are you, a mind reader?"

"No." He shrugged and his voice softened a notch. "But you're not difficult to read. Your face reflects things. Fears. Emotions. De—" He coughed and his voice edged back toward gruff. "I bet you're not much of a poker player."

She felt a faint smile touch her lips. "Dad gave up trying to teach me after a while." But he'd done it with good humor and they'd compromised on chess, which required deadly strategy and not much bluffing.

"You're close to him." It wasn't a question.

"Yes. He's a wonderful man. You'd—" *like him,* she started to say, but then broke off because Logan would never meet her father, because he was just passing through.

Her smile faded at the guilty realization that though Logan claimed to be able to read her, he hadn't guessed— or hadn't verbalized—the last part of her tension.

Him. The situation.

What sort of protective custody would his bosses provide? Would she even see him during the investigation, the trial?

Maybe it would be best if she didn't. Now, pressed together in the small truck cab, they created an energy that crackled over her skin and made her wish for impossible things.

They passed a sign for a rest area, and Sam thought maybe it was time for a break, for some distance, to breathe some air that didn't carry his scent, or the hint of char that reminded her of the bomb and her once-pretty rental kitchen.

As she signaled and eased off the highway, Logan's phone rang.

He pulled it from an inner pocket of his jacket. "Hart

here." There was a pause, and his voice softened to an unimaginably tender degree. "Nancy! Hey, darling, how are you?"

Nancy? Darling?

Roaring jealousy caught Sam square in the heart, stunning her with its intensity.

Logan glanced at her, then lowered his voice as though seeking privacy.

Fine. She'd let him have it. He deserved it, and she had no right to her anger. They weren't a couple, even though they had kissed with a passion that defied description.

Rage spiked in Sam's gut. He could kiss her like that, then soften his voice so achingly when he talked to some bimbo named Nancy?

She knew she was overreacting, but couldn't help it. Thankful that they'd reached the rest stop, she parked the truck, shut it off and leaped out. "I'll leave you to your conversation."

"Hold on." His hand shot out and grabbed her wrist. "Wait for me." He covered the receiver and dropped his voice. "They might have followed us here."

Interesting. He didn't want his girlfriend to know about the danger. Then again, could she blame him? She didn't even want to know about it, and she was smack-dab in the middle of the bloody situation.

She shook him off. "I'll be fine." She gestured behind her to the other cars, the bright lights that illuminated the parking area against the fading dusk. "Nothing will happen to me here."

After a moment, he nodded, uncovered the phone and dropped his voice back to that tone he'd never once directed toward Sam. "Sorry. I'm back. What was that?" His eyes cut to her, then away. "Business, Nance. Just business."

As she walked from the truck to the busy rest stop, Sam told herself not to be petty, that she had no claim on the handsome M.D., that they'd made no promises to each other, not even an implied understanding beyond that one kiss. It wasn't until after she grabbed a handful of prepackaged snacks and a couple of sodas that she realized that the hot, black emotion in her gut wasn't pure jealousy, wasn't just a catty hiss that someone else owned the man she might have wanted to call her own for a night or two—

It was envy. A far more complex emotion.

She wanted, not just Logan, but what he had with the woman on the other end of the phone—a relationship so clearly defined in the tone of his voice, in the softness of his replies and the almost complete absence of his customary gruffness when he'd spoken to her.

Love.

The single word caught her in the chest like a blow, and she had to remind herself to breathe. For two years, ever since she and Louie had split, she'd told herself she wasn't lonely, that her friends and her father gave her everything she needed.

But what if she'd been lying to herself? What then?

"You okay?" Logan's voice at her shoulder was a jolt, the rush of warmth an uncomfortable reminder.

She shifted away. "Fine. You want anything else?" She lifted her choices, having picked a few things for him based on what she'd seen in the wreckage of her kitchen.

The thought added a tremble of nerves to her general upset.

"What you have is fine." He paid for the snacks over her protest and led the way back to the truck, darting glances into the shadows as though daring Trehern's men to try for her. But there was no sign of deadly danger.

Not yet.

Logan took the wheel and Sam didn't bother arguing. He looked sharp enough, and the greater part of her wanted to curl up into a ball and wait until the day was over. Maybe the week. Hell, even a month, because who knew how long this would take?

A month under Logan Hart's protection. The idea was as frightening as it was thrilling.

"That was my sister," he said abruptly into the tense silence. At her guilty flinch, he glanced over, then away. "Nancy. My sister." He shrugged. "I just thought you should know that."

Relief shivered through her, followed by new tension. Then shame for her nasty thoughts. But over it all, the tension. "Why?"

She wanted him to be the one to acknowledge the kiss, to say there was an attraction between them that neither could deny.

Instead of answering, he stared through the windshield at the lamp-lit road that would take them to the city. "Her husband, Stephen, works for HFH as an infectious-disease specialist. They send him places sometimes. This last time, he didn't come home."

Instant empathy and a sharper flare of guilt pierced Sam. She'd been so caught up in the flurry of activity and danger surrounding her over the past few days, she hadn't really stopped to consider that Logan had a life outside of Black Horse Beach.

Maybe she hadn't wanted to.

But though she was an only child, she could imagine Logan's worry on his sister's behalf. Worse, she could hear a hint of it in his voice, see a slice of pain in his cool expression.

The kernel of vulnerability in Logan's expression touched a chord, and Sam felt a stab of pain for his sister. She knew how it felt to watch a man walk away after things were said and done. How much worse could it be to have him disappear when the love was still strong?

She shifted on the bench seat. "I'm sorry."

He nodded, then continued, jaw tight. "He's been gone a little over three months. Yesterday, a ransom demand arrived. They're waiting for proof that he's still alive."

His fingers flexed on the steering wheel like he wanted to lash out, and she couldn't blame him. Of course he wanted to be there with her. Family was family. And though she'd never consciously considered what his life might be like away from Black Horse Beach, it didn't surprise her to learn that he was close to his family.

Unfortunately, it made her like him more, and she couldn't afford to do that.

She crossed her arms and settled back against the seat, wishing she could do something more helpful than repeat, "I'm sorry."

"Don't be. It's not your fault I rented your cottage, led hired killers to your door and pretty much ruined your life." Before she could contradict him, he ground out, "It's my fault. Mine and Trehern's."

"More Trehern's than yours," she argued. "You didn't ask him to be a criminal."

"Yes, but I put myself in the line of fire, just like Stephen did. And neither of us thought about the collateral damage." His words went ragged, though he fought them back to gruff before she could comment. He shot her a sidelong glance. "That's not the sort of thing it's fair to ask a woman to put up with."

And then she got it. This was his roundabout way of telling her there was no future for them. For all his harsh manners, Logan was trying to do the right thing.

The sting of rejection was foolish, Sam told herself. She'd planned on telling him that she had no intention of becoming involved with another he-man who would never settle in a small town. Her heart couldn't stand doing that again.

And she had a feeling that if she and Logan tried an

affair, the inevitable crash would be worse than any of the others she'd experienced. So why risk it?

She was trying to be smarter these days.

He glanced over again and she shook her head and put him out of his misery. "Don't worry. I get it. And if it's any help, I was preparing this whole speech about why it was a bad idea for us to get involved, too."

"Oh. Good." He didn't look as relieved as she'd expected, and she didn't feel as relieved as she'd expected, either, especially when he signaled a turn off the expressway into Chinatown, shot her a glance and said, "And what about down on the beach? The kiss?"

Her face flamed as she remembered the torrid embrace. "We'll just forget it happened."

Which was a little like trying to ignore a giant schnauzer sitting in the centerpiece of a fancy-dress dinner. Impossible.

His molten look said the same, but aloud he said, "Good. Then this shouldn't be a problem."

He sent the truck into an enclosed parking garage. The walls echoed to silence as he parked near a key-coded elevator lobby and killed the engine.

Sam shivered slightly at the sudden quiet and the grim darkness of the parking garage. "What won't be a problem?"

He slid from the truck and reached back in for both of their suitcases. "My bosses and I have agreed that you'll be safest in the suite with me. You'll have your own room, and we'll share the bathroom and the kitchen. But that won't be a problem, seeing as we've agreed that we'll simply ignore the attraction. Right?"

His narrow-eyed stare and tense shoulders suggested that he might have been as offended by her quick agreement as she'd been by his well-camouflaged brush-off. But Sam couldn't deal with that right then. Her brain was too full of the buzzing words *share the bathroom and the kitchen.*

Hell, no!

She couldn't share a suite with him. Impossible! They'd see each other in the morning. At night. At odd hours in between as they, and the HFH operatives he'd promised for help, searched for Trehern's hired guns.

Her door opened abruptly, nearly sending her to the asphalt. Logan braced her with a strong hand, then stepped away and extended that same hand as though asking for her decision. "Okay?"

No, it wasn't okay. The whole situation was anything but okay. But she found herself nodding and taking his hand, letting him lead her to the elevators and watching while he keyed in a code.

The security lock flashed green, he opened the door and gestured her through—

And a cool, deadly voice spoke from behind them both. "Welcome home, Doc. I've been waiting for you."

HELL! LOGAN SHOVED Sam through the door and spun toward the voice, damning himself for the lapse. He should've been paying better attention, should have been searching the shadows rather than worrying about his and Sam's not-gonna-happen relationship. He snapped over his shoulder, "Take the elevator upstairs and call Security."

A figure stepped from the deep shadows behind the elevator, where a bulb had burned out. Or, Logan realized now, been shot out.

Viggo was nothing if not thorough, and expected his men to be the same.

"No elevator. No Security." The smooth voice brought back memories, as did the sight of William Caine, Trehern's trusted lieutenant.

William was about Logan's height and weight, about his age. By looks, the two men could have been brothers. Oddly, they could have been friends, as well. They had been, once, but that friendship had been based on a lie.

Logan's lie. And he saw the anger of it, the betrayal of it, sharp in the other man's normally cold eyes. Though he'd been jailed in the same raid as his boss, William had turned minimal evidence in exchange for his freedom. At the time, Logan had hoped he'd decided to go straight.

Now he knew. William was out for revenge against the man who had been instrumental in destroying his employer. His way of life.

Logan was dead. He and Sam were both dead.

Spurred by the thought, by desperation, he yelled, "Sam, run!"

He leaped at William and pulled his weapon, hoping

surprise, or maybe their false friendship would slow the other man's response. But there was no such luck. Trehern's man sidestepped and kicked the gun out of his hand. Logan reversed direction, determined to keep his own body between Samantha and William while she escaped.

Trehern's assassin closed in, but didn't pull a gun. This was pure hand-to-hand combat. Logan had some formal training, and had picked up twice as much informal experience since enlisting with HFH, but he knew William had been born into middle-class obscurity and had clawed his way into the tight ranks of Trehern's empire through fighting skills and sheer tenacity. He was reputed to know every pressure point in the human body. With one touch, he could knock a man out for a minute or an hour.

Or permanently.

With a growl, William bared his teeth and leaped forward.

"Logan, look out!"

He didn't need Sam's scream to know she hadn't followed his orders, hadn't escaped upstairs while he bought her precious time. "Damn it, Sam, get out of here!"

He crouched and got in a lucky blow, driving his shoulder into William's gut hard enough to knock the breath out of the other man.

"I've called 911," she said loudly. "The police will be here any minute."

William sucked in a breath on a raspy chuckle, but

he didn't look worried. They both knew cell signals were nonexistent in parking garages. "Gutsy, isn't she?" He feinted at Logan's jaw with his left hand, then swung hard with his right and connected.

Logan's vision blurred as he reeled away. He struck out blindly and connected with a solid smack of flesh on flesh. "Stay away from her, you bastard."

"I'm not interested in her. At least, not directly." William was panting now. Blood trickled from a split lip and from a gash above his eyebrow.

Logan saw the change in his eyes, saw them go from cool blue to disinterested ice.

The way they'd changed just before Viggo shot Sharilee, as though William had known something awful was about to happen, didn't like it, but didn't care enough to stop it. Logan braced himself for a bullet.

He got a fist to the jaw.

Sam screamed. Logan stumbled back, spun, then howled when William's arm snaked across his throat.

Then he didn't have the breath left to howl as William tightened his grip and Logan's windpipe folded.

"Let go of him!" He heard footsteps running toward them and yelled inside his head, *Sam, get out of here! Go!*

He didn't want her to see this. It had never been her fight.

When William shifted his grip to one-handed and reached into his pocket, Logan drove his heel into the other man's shin and shot an elbow back. He didn't get free, but the arm across his throat loosened enough for him to rasp, "Leave me! Run!"

"No." There was a click at Logan's temple as William continued, "She should stay. This involves both of you."

Logan froze, eyes locked on Sam's stricken expression. But even as he wished with fervid intensity that he'd never left the city, never rented the pretty cottage on Black Horse Beach, his mind asked one insistent question.

If William was armed, why the fistfight?

"The bloody nose was for me," the other man said calmly, his thought patterns having mirrored Logan's as accurately as they had before, when the men had been friends separated by differing agendas, "this is for my former employer."

Punishment before he died, Logan realized, then braced himself for the shot.

Rapid-fire emotions flared in his gut. Regret for the things he'd done, the things he hadn't done. Sadness for Nancy, who would probably never see Stephen again. Pain for Samantha, who would be haunted by his execution just as he'd been haunted by Sharilee's murder.

Fear. Gut-numbing fear.

But the shot never came.

After a moment, William chuckled dryly in his ear. "Had you scared, didn't I?" He pressed a folded paper into Logan's hand. "This is from Viggo Jr. He wants you to bugger off."

And the arm across Logan's throat and the gun at his temple were gone.

Logan stumbled forward into Sam, then scooped his fallen weapon and crouched, ready for another attack.

But Trehern's enforcer had been swallowed up by the darkness near the shot-out light. Moments later, a well-tuned engine purred to life and the sleek shape of a pricey sedan disappeared from the garage.

God, Logan thought in that instant, *thank you, God*.

Then a wash of shame hit him, along with the sure knowledge that he could have handled that better. He could have fought harder, smarter. But in his brain, William was irrevocably connected to the moment of Sharilee's death, to the horrible things he'd seen. Worse, a piece of him still thought of William as a friend.

Part of him had fought, true. But part of him had frozen, and Sam could have paid the price.

"Logan." She touched his arm. "Let's get inside." Only a slight tremor betrayed her fear.

"Okay." He herded her through the coded door into the relative safety of the elevator lobby, and pressed the button—normal actions, everyday actions that had little to do with the raw, fatalistic terror of the past few minutes.

He'd thought he was dead, and Sam, too.

He'd gone to Black Horse Beach to heal, but everything that had happened served to point out one irrevocable truth—that he hadn't healed at all. He'd simply avoided the memories.

The doors dinged with painful cheer. He gestured her inside the elevator and breathed in relief when the metal slabs glided shut, insulating them. Protecting them.

The building was owned by Boston General, having been deeded to the hospital by head administrator Zach Cage right after he married his wife, Dr. Ripley Davis. Cage had bought the building back when he'd been a professional baseball player, and it had all the amenities that came with status—including security in the lobby and coded locks on every door. Above the garage level, it was secure.

He hoped.

"Logan? Are you okay?" Sam's worried eyes fastened on his face. "Are you hurt? Who was that man?"

"No, I'm not hurt." He flexed his fingers into fists and was almost startled to feel paper crumple. He'd all but forgotten about the note. "And that was William Caine. He works for Trehern."

But he'd said the message came from Viggo Jr., which meant the organization was alive and well and under the rulership of Viggo's son. Damn it. Just damn it.

The beginnings of failure echoed hollowly in Logan's chest. Had he given up eighteen months, had Sharilee given up her *life* only so they could jail one ruler and crown another in his place?

Hell, what a mess.

"What does the note say?" Sam asked quietly, as though understanding he wouldn't tell her unless she pressed, that he wanted to keep her as far away from Trehern's horror as possible, though it seemed less and less possible with each passing day.

He met her eyes then, and felt a punch of power at the connection. A punch of power and a spurt of fear. William was smart. Too smart. If there had been any doubt in the organization about Logan and Sam's relationship, it was gone now that William had seen them together.

Logan had no power to hide his reaction to her, his consuming need to protect her, to keep her safe.

To keep her near.

"Logan? The note?"

As that final realization shivered through him, he couldn't deny that bringing her to the city had as much to do with what he wanted as it did with what was best for her.

Rocked by the treacherous emotions, he unclenched his fingers and looked down at the crumpled white envelope. Edged with a thin ribbon of burgundy and gold, it looked expensive. Classy. Legitimate.

Much like Trehern himself, it wasn't until he looked beneath the surface that the evil became clear.

The elevator car rose smoothly to the lobby and the doors eased open so they could check in at the security desk before taking a second lift to the penthouse suite.

But Sam and Logan remained in the elevator. After a moment, the doors glided shut once more, shutting them in together.

Logan broke the seal on the envelope and pulled out the single sheet of linen paper, which was embossed with the intertwined letters V and T, and the image of an arching tree. Hidden within the logo was a serpent with wickedly pointed fangs.

Again, evil hidden within seeming class.

Sam didn't ask again, understanding that he needed a moment, that this wasn't anything he wanted to get involved with. Not again.

Then, damning himself for the delay, Logan unfolded the sheet of paper, where a single sentence punched him in the gut and left him reeling.

I didn't order the hit.

Chapter Seven

"What the hell does that mean?" Upset, Sam shoved her trembling hands in her pockets. "Who didn't send what?"

"I think Viggo Jr. wants me to know he didn't send the assassin." Logan stared down at the paper as though force of will might make more words appear. He scowled darkly. "But if that's the case, then why tell me? And who *did* send the shooter?"

When he glanced at her, she shrugged. "Beats me."

The elevator doors opened once again. This time, he gestured her into the lobby. "Come on. Let's check in with Security and head upstairs. I have some calls to make."

Sam followed, feeling more than ever that she was along for the ride here, that at all times someone else was making the decisions for her, that she was the puppet and someone else was yanking her strings.

She bloody well hated the feeling, but didn't think digging in her heels would help. She was Sheriff Bob's daughter, true, but she didn't have the foggiest clue what was going on. When the man in the garage had grabbed Logan, she'd wanted to do something, anything to help, but she'd been powerless.

She hated that feeling, too. In fact, she hated this whole situation. She hated that Logan had come into her life, disrupted her normally peaceful existence and dragged her into the city for her own protection only to find the danger had followed them.

Or maybe it had waited for them.

God, she should have stayed home. She could be in the clinic right now, working with Maverick, trying to show the dog that not all humans were bad. Instead, she was here, amid the bad humans in the city while Jimmy kept watch over Jen at the clinic.

Anger was a low-grade itch as Sam followed Logan to a second set of elevators. They rode up in a silence broken only by the rustle of expensive paper as he reread the note and cursed low.

But she had a feeling he didn't need to reread the single line of text. He was avoiding her.

And with good reason. He'd come into her life and turned it upside down. She would be angry with him except that he was so obviously upset.

He hadn't meant for any of this to happen. Yet it had, and now they needed to deal with it.

They entered the opulent penthouse suite together, though Sam barely glanced at the rich chrome and leather furnishings and the wide windows that revealed the sweeping Boston skyline and a glitter of water.

She spun on him, intending to relieve some of her

fear and frustration, part of the roiling uncertainty that she chose to call anger. But before she could frame a complaint, or maybe a question, the words backed up in her throat at the look of torture on his face.

He stood in the entryway, paper and envelope dangling from one hand, and looked lost. Absolutely lost.

"I need to tell you about Trehern. About Sharilee. Then maybe you'll understand how I know this is all part of a big game to him."

Any jealousy Sam might have felt at the woman's name and the emotion behind it was burned away by Logan's quiet grief. The rough rasp of his voice was oddly atonal, as though all the emotion had been pushed out of him. But his eyes were all emotion, lit with guilt and sadness, shadowed with the recent fight.

And a quiet plea.

Softening, Sam gestured him to a stiff black couch that proved to be butter-soft. "Sit. Tell me."

When he sat, she checked him over and found sore spots but no breaks, no real bleeding. He'd been lucky.

Or the other man had pulled his punches.

Part of Sam knew they should call the cops, or maybe Logan's bosses, and report the incident in the garage. But all the reports in the world hadn't helped yet, and it was clear Logan needed to talk.

Besides, she wanted to hear what he had to say, needed to hear it, because maybe it would help her understand what was happening and why.

What would come next.

"Tell me."

He drew in a ragged breath. "The feds hadn't been able to get Viggo on anything important, not really. He'd beaten charges ranging from murder to extortion and everything in between. So they started looking at the relatively unimportant things, and realized he had a fondness for prescription drugs. That was something the feds could prosecute on, so they contacted HFH and asked for a joint team. HFH agreed to send me in as a doctor and the feds agreed to send in an operative as backup. Only they wouldn't tell me who it was."

His voice had gone cold, distant, as though reciting facts he'd told a thousand times. Sam supposed he had done just that, in debriefings and trial prep. But it was the grief behind the cold that grabbed her. Warned her.

His phone rang in his jacket pocket, but he seemed not to hear it. When it fell silent after five rings, she urged, "Go on."

He jolted and she saw the memories crowding his eyes. Dark memories.

"My cover played on the fact that I had been arrested as a suspect for a series of murders in BoGen's transplant department." Sam looked at him in surprise and a wry smile twisted his lips. "Yeah, a suspect. We had a pair of HFH operatives working on the murders. It turned out that my boss had bloody well framed me, when all along it was him selling BoGen transplant organs to the highest bidder." He paused. "Anyway, that was my introduction to HFH."

His expression held a poignant mix of pride and regret. It hit Sam hard in the chest, because she recognized it. Her father looked like that when he spoke of his wife, and the career choices that had driven her away.

Sam's mother had wanted bright lights and fast city nights. Her father's calling had been Black Horse Beach.

There hadn't been any middle ground.

But this wasn't about Sam's father, and it wasn't about the tight ache in her chest at the sight of Logan's face, or the stab of worry that speared through her at the thought that he'd gone undercover to bring down a man the feds had been unable to catch.

It was about his choices and how they'd come full circle.

He continued, "We used that jail time as a hook to get me in with Viggo, and played up the suspicion that I'd been involved in the organ-selling scheme." He glanced at her, the first time he'd truly looked at her since sitting down on the couch. "I hadn't been, of course, but there was no way they'd look at a squeaky-clean doctor who'd graduated at the top of his class, moved straight into transplant medicine at BoGen and flirted with a few top-ten-bachelor lists."

The image of a young, upwardly mobile doctor was so far from the gruff, unhappy man sitting near her that Sam wasn't quite sure what to say.

He spread his hands. "Anyway, it took some doing, but I eventually established myself as one of Trehern's most trusted doctors. I got him the prescription drugs he wanted and he kept me close. Too close, sometimes."

His face reflected what must have been a horrible year and a half. Sam didn't even want to imagine it, but couldn't stop the images from forming in her brain. She eased closer on the couch and touched his knee. "You don't have to tell me this."

He took a deep breath. "Who better? You've been dragged into this, so it's only fair you understand a bit of what's going on." He looked down at her hand on his knee, then covered it with his own.

The contact brought a shock of electricity, then a low hum of warmth.

Bad idea, she told herself. *Very bad idea.*

But she didn't move away.

He continued, "When the end came, it was quick. I'd collected all the evidence we needed, and HFH and the feds were getting ready to pull me out. At the same time, they were going to pull out the undercover fed who'd been sent in to back me up. They'd never told me who it was—they didn't trust I wouldn't break the other guy's cover." He glanced at her. "I always thought it was William. He seemed decent, and had a good sense of humor. Damn it, I even liked him!"

There was venom in the last sentence, a tired anger as though he'd beaten himself up over the friendship already and had laid that demon mostly to rest.

"What happened?"

His fingers tightened on her hand. "Even to this day,

I'm not entirely sure. We were three days from dropping the hammer when it happened. Viggo got it in his head that he had a leak in the organization, and he called a meeting." Logan's eyes darkened. "There was a woman. Some bimbo he'd picked up at a bar and kept around for fun. I'd never had much to do with her, because Viggo was territorial." He took a breath. "He shot her. Right in front of us. It happened so fast, I couldn't stop it. I didn't even try."

"Oh, God." Sam's stomach knotted.

"It gets worse." He pulled his hand away and stood. Began to pace. "The feds heard the shot over the wire I was wearing and busted in not five minutes later. Nobody saw it coming. But it turned out that she'd been my backup. She was a damned fed." His hands fisted and relaxed at his sides. "That shouldn't make it worse—a life is a life, a death is a death. But it *was* worse." He looked at her. "As they dragged the others out, I went a little nuts, screaming and cursing and trying to revive her, even though the back of her head was gone. Viggo saw that and he got this little smile on his face, as though I'd just given him a precious gift. And I had." His eyes were molten now, with guilt and self-recrimination. "He knew how to hurt me now—by hurting a woman. He's smart enough to know it'll be worse if he hurts someone I know."

Understanding shivered through her. She'd known the danger before, it had been hard to ignore with bullets flying around and her truck at the bottom of the ocean, but the perpetrator had been obscure to her, a faceless menace that Logan had brought with him.

Now, Trehern had a face. An ugly one.

"What about your sister?" If anyone could be used against Logan, it was Nancy, the woman he'd spoken to so softly, so kindly. With so much love.

Even now, the memory tugged at her.

"I convinced her and Stephen to move onto a military base for the duration of the trial. She was safe there, even when…" He trailed off as though considering something for the first time, then shook his head. "No, no. Not even Trehern could have arranged for him to be taken in Tehru. That's reaching." Logan returned to the couch and sat down beside Sam, close beside her, and took both of her hands. "But when they tracked me to Black Horse Beach…when they saw us talking at your front door… that gave them leverage. *I* gave them leverage."

And finally she understood that the darkness in his eyes, the guilt and the grief wasn't from a woman he'd loved and lost, but from a teammate he'd failed to protect.

Someone he didn't even know.

But when she mentally coupled that with the disappearance of his sister's husband, the story got a whole bunch clearer.

Logan was trying to protect her. Not just from Trehern, but from him, from the danger he represented in his own mind.

And perhaps he was trying to protect himself, as well.

Something shifted in her chest. Warmth bloomed,

laced through with a twist of regret as she realized that Logan was a man worthy of her respect.

She genuinely liked him, damn it, which only made the situation more difficult.

She'd loved her exes, but she hadn't always liked them. What would happen if she let herself care for a man like Logan, a man she not only desired, but also liked and respected?

A man whose work would require him to leave. A man with a worthy career, one she couldn't ever ask him to deny.

Heartbreak. That was the simple answer. Heartbreak.

The phone in his pocket rang again, startling them both so they jumped away from each other on the couch. Only then did she realize how close together they'd been. How near an embrace. A mistake.

He flipped the phone open and cleared his throat. "Hello?" After a moment of listening, he shifted his voice to crisp and businesslike. "Yeah, we're here. And we had a visitor in the garage. William Caine. He had a message for us." Logan paused, then nodded. "See you in ten."

"Your boss?" Sam asked, aware that the moment was past, the conversation over, yet not over at all. She wanted to know more about Logan, about his experiences undercover and whether he thought he could ever leave the work, ever be the committed young doctor with the bright future he'd described.

But she wouldn't ask, because she didn't need to

know. It wasn't important, because as soon as the killers were caught and Trehern jailed, she'd be on her way back to Black Horse Beach, and he'd be on his way to…wherever.

He nodded. "Zach Cage. I'm surprised he doesn't have the others with him, but I'm sure they're on their way."

Only they weren't.

"WHAT DO YOU MEAN I don't get any backup?" Disregarding seniority and protocol, Logan got right in Cage's face. "Someone's trying to kill us!"

Cage didn't even flinch. The darkly handsome hospital administrator gripped Logan's shoulder. "The Chinatown cops will help, and we've got building security so tight that not even a roach can get in. But as for outside manpower, I'm tapped."

Impossible. HFH had a dozen pairs of high-level operatives on the payroll and ten times that in ancillary staff. There was no way they were all unavailable, unless…

Unless something big was going down.

Something like a rescue effort.

Logan froze. Hell. "You're going in after Stephen."

Sam's gasp echoed in the wide room, and Cage neither confirmed nor denied Logan's guess. He merely gestured to the couch. "Let's sit and make a plan."

Logan sat, pulling Sam down beside him, not because there weren't enough chairs, but because he bloody well wanted her beside him. He'd never told anyone else the full story of what had happened that night in Trehern's mansion—at least not what he'd felt about it.

Sure, he'd recited the facts a hundred times, but he'd never before admitted his feelings of failure.

He'd failed Sharilee. He should have been smarter, quicker. But he hadn't been, and she'd died with a surprised look on her face and his hands on her chest as he tried to keep her heart alive long after her body had failed.

Sam sat beside him without protest. She didn't touch him, but her warmth was a reminder that he couldn't be two places at once. He couldn't protect her and save Stephen both.

But still…

"I don't suppose you're going to let me fly to Tehru, are you?" Even before Cage shook his head in the negative, another thought occurred. "God, you didn't let Nancy fly over, did you?"

He wanted to be there when she got the news, good or bad. He wanted to be there to hold her, to cheer if the news was good. And if it wasn't…

He needed to be there.

"Of course not." Cage looked mildly disgusted. "I'm not an idiot. She's on the base. I'd have brought her here, except for this mess Trehern has organized. So I need you to pull yourself together, take a breath, and tell me what the hell's going on. Is it Trehern or not? Because Detective Peters and Sturgeon swear none of the organization's usual thugs have gone missing. So either we're dealing with a new hired gun, or something else is up."

"Of course it's Trehern," Logan snapped, irritated. But Sam's warmth at his back made him pause a moment and remember the note.

What if it was genuine? What if it wasn't Viggo or his son?

What then?

Then someone else was trying to kill him and Sam, and they had no backup, and no other theories.

Wordlessly, he handed over the note.

Cage frowned and read aloud. "I didn't order the hit." He glanced at Logan. "Do you have any reason to believe that Viggo Jr. is telling the truth?"

He'd thought about it briefly. "Not really. But at the same time, why would he lie? If they've sent men after me, then it's for one of two reasons—to threaten me into not testifying, or to kill me so I can't."

Sam stiffened at the baldness of the statement, and Logan had to restrain himself from throwing an arm across her shoulders to comfort her, or perhaps comfort them both. But that was a bad idea. She didn't need him confusing her life any more than he already had.

And his life was such a mess, any more confusion might make it implode.

Cage glanced at the note again, as though he, too, wished that another sentence or two would magically appear. "What about the delivery boy?"

"William." A faint smile touched Logan's lips, the ghost of a respect he hadn't yet managed to kill. Damn, he wished they were on the same team. They could have been friends. "I wouldn't exactly call him an errand boy. More like a pit bull on a mission." Which made him think of Sam's neighbor and the fighting dogs.

Black Horse Beach and its local problems seemed so far away. Strangely, part of him missed it, missed the quiet and the hiss of waves on the sand. The rhythm of the town and a morning cup of coffee with people who weren't quite strangers anymore. But missing it didn't mean he intended to return.

In fact, it would probably be kinder if he didn't.

"Can you find William? Can you get more information about Viggo Jr. and how much of the old organization he's taken over?" Cage's eyes asked a different set of questions.

Are you strong enough to go back there? Will you?

Logan gritted his teeth. If Cage had asked him the question a week ago, the answer would have been a re-sounding no. Though he intended to go back to field-work eventually, he never again wanted to be undercover that deep for that long. Besides, he would need to be careful. William knew who he was and wanted something. What of the others? This could so easily become a trap.

But with Sam's life in danger…

He exhaled. "If that's what it takes. Yeah, I can find him."

"Good. Then do it." Cage stood, holding the note by the corner. "I'll take this over to the Chinatown station. They know the basics of what's happened so far. Walk with me and I'll tell you what I can about the rescue before you leave."

That confirmed Logan's hunch. HFH was going into Tehru after his brother-in-law. God, how could he be so separated from the event? How could he not be there when Nancy needed him?

He glanced over at Sam, knowing he was needed equally as much here. More so, because this was his mess.

His and Sam's.

She rose from the couch when he did, and walked to the door with the men. Cage went ahead and waited at the elevators, giving them a discreet moment Logan wasn't sure he wanted.

It would have been easier just to leave. But it wouldn't have been fair.

He turned to her, lifted a hand to stroke her cheek then let it fall to his side, knowing he shouldn't touch her at all. "You'll be safe in here. Don't leave the penthouse and don't let anyone up. I'll be back in a few hours."

He expected her eyes to flash with annoyance, or maybe defiance, but she simply nodded. "I won't. Don't worry about me."

But he would, damn it. Every moment he was away from her, he'd wonder whether she was okay. Whether she was still in the penthouse or had gone off on her own.

She wasn't the sort to stay meekly behind.

"Promise me," he pushed. "Promise you won't leave the penthouse until I get back."

She surprised him by nodding. "I promise." Then her eyes softened, her voice dropped. "Go find William Caine and don't worry about me. I'll stay put. This time."

This time. He felt his lips quirk at the modifier that told him exactly what he'd suspected, that Sam had no intentions of sitting idly by while the others worked to find the assassins.

"Thank you." He touched his lips to hers before either of them was prepared for it. The jolt of electrical current was way out of proportion for a simple touch, and Logan saw his own surprise mirrored in her eyes when he pulled back. "Sorry," he said, "bad idea."

"Yeah." She nodded and touched a hand to her throat. "Real bad idea." She took a step away. "Be careful, okay?"

He lingered a moment more, not quite ready to step outside the richly furnished penthouse and descend back to the place that had become his own personal hell. Then the elevators dinged in the hallway and Cage cleared his throat.

It was time to go.

Logan wanted to drag Sam into his arms and kiss her properly. He wanted to promise her something she could hold him to when he got back, though he had no idea what it might be. He wanted to turn his back on Cage, shut the door and take her to bed, bury himself inside her and tell himself the rest of it would go away if they locked the penthouse and never came out.

He wanted…God, he didn't know what the hell he wanted anymore. Didn't even know who he was.

Get FREE BOOKS and a FREE GIFT when you play the...

LAS VEGAS GAME

Just scratch off the gold box with a coin. Then check below to see the gifts you get! →

YES! I have scratched off the gold box. Please send me my **2 FREE BOOKS** and **gift for which I qualify.** I understand that I am under no obligation to purchase any books as explained on the back of this card.

382 HDL D7Z6   **182 HDL D7YW**

FIRST NAME

LAST NAME

ADDRESS

APT.#

CITY

STATE/PROV.

ZIP/POSTAL CODE

(H-I-06/05)

7	7	7	Worth TWO FREE BOOKS plus a BONUS Mystery Gift!
🍒	🍒	🍒	Worth TWO FREE BOOKS!
🔔	🔔	♣	TRY AGAIN!

www.eHarlequin.com

Offer limited to one per household and not valid to current Harlequin Intrigue® subscribers. All orders subject to approval.

So he turned on his heel and left without another word, feeling the warmth stay behind in the penthouse with Sam.

In the elevator, Cage briefly sketched out the plan for rescuing Stephen. It was simple, full of holes and hinged on cooperation with one of the least predictable factions involved in the current Tehruvian civil war.

Poor Nancy, Logan thought. Then he remembered his phone. "Here." As the elevator reached the ground floor and the men stepped out, he pulled the phone from his inner pocket and handed it to Cage, unwilling to bring the familial link when he went to find William. "Have the security guard bring this up to Sam, will you? Better yet, take it yourself. I made her promise not to let anyone into the suite."

"Sure." Cage took the phone, then gripped Logan's shoulder. "You sure you're okay with this?"

"What choice have you left me?" But Logan's question held little bitterness. There was no better plan and they both knew it.

And Cage knew some of what had happened, some of how it had made Logan feel. Because of it, he'd put Logan on an enforced vacation for the duration of the trial.

That the time away had been a disaster was no fault of Cage's. The blame rested squarely on Viggo and his organization.

Because of it, Logan returned Cage's gesture. "I'll be fine."

"Call me as soon as you get back to the penthouse,

okay? Better yet, take this with you." Cage handed him an operations phone. One of HFH's neatest gadgets, it was fitted with everything from a global-positioning tracker to a small explosive charge with a miniature timer.

"Thanks." Logan tucked the unit into his inner jacket pocket and felt a measure of security. He hadn't carried such things undercover—they would have marked him as an operative.

Carrying one now took him one degree away from the man he'd become in Trehern's employ.

"Good luck." Cage sketched a wave and returned to the elevator so he could bring Sam the phone.

Logan could have brought it to her himself, but he'd said his goodbye already. Seeing her again would only make it harder.

So he took the second elevator down to the garage and was careful to watch the shadows as he unlocked the truck. He slid onto the bench seat, shut the door and fired the engine.

A voice spoke from the back seat. "Looking for me?"

Logan's gut iced as a gun barrel pressed into the skin behind his ear for the second time that night. "William." The name was barely a whisper.

The other man's voice dropped to ice. "We need to talk, but not here. Drive."

Logan's heart thumped double-time and cool sweat prickled as fear washed over him. He'd wanted to meet with William, true, but not here. Not like this.

Not with Sam so close by.

Intent on getting away from her, he slammed the transmission into reverse and navigated out of the parking space using only the rearview mirror. Blood hammered in his ears, his legs vibrated with the desire to run. Escape. "Where are we going?"

"I'll tell you when we get there."

Chapter Eight

Sam held it together until the door shut behind Cage for the second time, leaving her standing alone in the grand apartment with Logan's cell phone in her hand.

It was still warm and she fancied it was from his body heat. She touched the small device to her cheek and prayed for his safety.

She could deal with veterinary emergencies in the middle of the night, with prissy pets, obnoxious owners, and even with Horace Mann and his shotgun. But she didn't know how to deal with this situation, didn't know how she could possibly help.

Logan was on his way back to a place that had wounded him deeply. She had sensed it in his expression when he'd talked about his time undercover, she'd heard it in his voice. He didn't want to go back there. But he was doing exactly that. For her safety. For his.

In this, but in nothing else, they were a couple.

"Urgh!" Frustrated with her thoughts, and the way they kept circling back time and again to the taste of his kiss and the press of his body, she turned away from the door and forced herself into the kitchen, where she started a pot of coffee.

It was going to be a long night.

While the coffee perked, she flipped open her own phone and dialed home.

The clinic line rang. And rang. And rang. Panic gathered beneath her breastbone and bubbled to the surface. Oh, God! Something had happened to Jennifer. She was hurt, she'd been kidnapped, she—

"Hello?" The voice was breathless and laced with a giggle.

"Jennifer?" Worry gave over to instant confusion. "What's going on?" The rumble of a familiar male voice served only to increase Sam's bewilderment. "Is somebody there with you? Are you okay?"

To her knowledge, Jen hadn't looked at a man since escaping her marriage. She'd focused on getting healthy, on getting stronger. On making a new life. So what the hell was going on?

"I'm fine." The lilt in Jen's voice was unfamiliar. Young. Almost sexy. "Jimmy and I are just finishing up the animals for the evening."

"Jimmy?" Always before, it had been *Sheriff Donahue* this and *Sheriff Donahue* that. Come to think of it, Jen had said the two words an awful lot, almost like a woman with a crush.

Or a woman in love.

What the hell was happening in Black Horse Beach?

Sam wondered. She had been gone for a day and her best friend had hooked up with her...other best friend?

She turned inward and looked for a spark of jealousy. She found only a faint sadness.

"Sam?" Jimmy's voice came on the line, not laughing, but also a little out of breath. "What's going on up there? Are you okay? Is Hart behaving himself?"

"I'm not sure you're in any position to ask that at the moment, James," she said with irritation borne of a twinge of envy. Then she stopped and took a breath. "Sorry."

There was silence on the other end, then Jimmy's voice, very serious. "Is this going to be a problem for us, Sam? I mean, I know you and I had talked about dating and all...but—"

"No problem," she interrupted firmly. "We discussed this the other day. It was never going to happen between us. On paper, we should have worked. But in real life, I think we make really, really good friends. Okay?"

His sigh of relief carried down the line. "Okay. That's what I thought, but I wanted to make sure. It's just that I've sort of had this thing for Jennie for a few years now, but with you and I circling around each other, and everything she's been through...well, when I ran into the clinic yesterday and thought for a moment that she'd been hurt, it let me know a few things. And one of those things was that it was time." His voice softened, and it was clear to Sam that he wasn't talking specifically to her anymore. "Lucky for me, Jen agreed."

There was a quiet moment. Sam imagined them kissing, and felt a phantom brush of lips across her own, an echo of electricity that quickly faded in the empty apartment.

When Jimmy came up for air, his voice shifted to that of the Black Horse sheriff. "So tell me what's up."

She sketched out what had happened that day, and where they stood, leaving out the parts about Logan's sister, because that information was private and it didn't relate to Trehern or the shooter. She ended by saying, "Is everything okay there? Have the state cops figured anything out?"

"Everything's fine," Jimmy answered. "You've only had a couple of calls—one from Izzy and one from that racetrack barn, Bellamy."

"Doc Sears called to apologize?" she asked, surprised.

"No. The farm manager. He asked where you were, but I played dumb. We're not telling anyone where you went, just in case. The guy didn't leave a message, so I guess it wasn't important."

Or they'd asked one of the vets farther north to help instead, Sam thought with a twist of dismay. Damn it! How had things gotten so complicated?

"Your truck's been salvaged," Jimmy continued, "though *salvage* may be an optimistic term. It's a real mess." Sam tried not to let the dollar signs add up in her head, but she winced nonetheless. Jimmy continued, "The brake lines were cut, all right. The funny thing is that the lab boys said it was a pretty messy job. Didn't look professional at all, which doesn't fit with what Logan said about Trehern's operation. Same with the shooting. We've dug slugs out of the front of your house that came nowhere near either of you."

A quiver of nerves strung itself through Sam's stomach. "What are you saying?"

"I'm not sure what I'm saying." Jimmy's frustration jangled down the line. "The evidence we have down here doesn't seem like it lines up with the information Logan's giving us."

"Meaning?"

"Meaning watch your back, okay? I'm not sure we have this all figured out yet."

A shiver worked down Sam's spine as Jimmy's hunch combined itself with the note Trehern's enforcer had delivered. "Same to you. Take care, and take care of Jen, too."

There was a new note in his voice when he said, "I will."

Sam disconnected the call and leaned up against the kitchen counter, coffee forgotten.

What if Trehern hadn't sent the killer? What then?

It meant that Logan had another enemy. One he wasn't watching out for. She didn't even bother to consider the alternative, because who would want to kill her?

She was nobody.

The phone rang at Sam's elbow, startling her. She grabbed it. "Hello?" As silence hummed on the line, she realized she'd just answered Logan's phone, not her own. She scrambled to cover the mistake. "Logan Hart's phone. May I help you?"

"This is his sister, Nancy. Who is this?" The soft, feminine voice held a hint of steel, a quiver of strain.

"You don't know me. My name is Samantha Black-well. I'm Logan's…landlady." That seemed a safe enough answer.

"Where's Logan?" The quiver became a crack. "He's not hurt, is he?"

"No," Sam answered quickly, "No, he's not hurt. He's…out. He'll be back in an hour or so." Please, God, let him be back in an hour or so. William Caine had seemed cold and fierce, not the sort of man to be torn by loyalty and friendship, as Logan was.

"Then I'm coming up."

The words took a moment to penetrate. Another moment to register. "You're what? Where are you?"

Cage had said Logan's sister was safe on the base. Far away. Nowhere near Boston, Viggo Trehern and his desire to punish Logan for crimes other people would consider justice.

"Downstairs in the lobby. Tell the guard to buzz me up, will you?" And the connection cut off before Sam could protest.

Don't let anyone up, Logan had said. He'd made her promise. But he couldn't have guessed his sister would fly in from the Midwest, could he?

He'd want her to let Nancy up. She was sure of it.

But even after Sam called downstairs and spoke with the guard, nerves feathered through her body.

She heard the cheerful ding of the elevator, heard the

doors slide open in the hallway, heard a footstep that sounded heavier that she'd expected.

Panic skittered through Sam's belly.

And she hoped to hell she hadn't made a huge mistake.

"PARK HERE," William said, using the muzzle of his gun to indicate a sand lot beneath an overpass. Probably a leftover from Baston's last construction project, it was deserted now, and dark from the concrete shadow above. The gun disappeared from Logan's peripheral view, though he knew it was nearby. William's voice ordered, "Get out and keep your hands where I can see them. I imagine you remember the drill."

There was a twist of resentment, of anger in the last.

Logan did as instructed, his gut churning with conflicting urges. Part of him wanted to punch William out, lunge back into the truck and drive away. But part of him knew this was why he'd left the apartment complex in the first place.

William had information he needed.

So he schooled himself to stillness as he slid from the truck and walked to the center of the black shadow beneath the overpass, hands well away from his body. Unarmed.

He'd thought about bringing his weapon, but knew William was faster on the draw and more accurate. More importantly, William could have shot him easily earlier that day.

But he hadn't. That told Logan the organization wanted him alive, not dead.

Which made no sense.

"Turn around." William's order came out of the deeper darkness near the concrete pylon.

Logan obeyed, feeling a light sweat break out across his lower back. He'd joined HFH looking for an excitement that he'd found lacking in transplant medicine, but this was more than he'd ever bargained for. More than he'd wanted.

And where the hell had that thought come from?

"Okay. You can chill." William waited for Logan to drop his hands and stand at ease before he said, "What do you want to know?"

The question startled Logan, though he tried not to let it show. There was something different about William tonight, though he couldn't quite pinpoint it. Didn't even try to as he asked, "Who is after me?"

"To my knowledge, nobody."

"Bull!" Logan took an aggressive step toward the other man's voice and pulled up short when a slice of headlight illumination from above glinted on the barrel of the semi-automatic. The overpass hummed with the passing vehicle, then fell silent.

In the distance, a church bell tolled the hour. Midnight.

Though motorists rolled along overhead, Logan felt very isolated. Just as he'd been undercover.

Some of the blackness he'd learned during that job descended on him and he stepped forward again, into

William's gun, until the muzzle pressed a small circle just beneath his heart. "Tell me who is trying to kill me, William. You know something, or you wouldn't have brought me that bogus note." He swallowed, the motion clicking against the strain in his throat. *"Who is trying to kill me?"*

"I told you. I. Don't. Know." William enunciated each word very clearly. "But it's not Viggo or Viggo Jr. Understand? It's not. I promise."

The last two words lit a raging fire within Logan, sparking off the twist of anger and the guilt of a death. "Why should I believe anything you say? Anything? You're a murderer and a thief, and turning state's evidence doesn't change that." He still couldn't believe they'd let William go in exchange for testimony. The betrayal burned, the memory of Sharilee's dead, staring eyes flared in his mind.

"Easy, Doc. You don't know everything."

The calm measure of his tone only served to enrage Logan further. He leaned in and shouted, "And now what? You're an errand boy for Viggo Jr.? His paid liar? Damn it, I liked you!" Ignoring the gun, he grabbed William by the collar and shook him. "Don't lie to me! Tell me who's trying to kill me!"

William dropped the gun, shoved Logan back with two hands, then punched him in the temple with a short, precisely placed chop.

Instant incapacitation.

Logan's legs folded beneath him, his vision dimmed from shadows to night, and he fell to the sand.

THE FOOTSTEPS in the elevator lobby weren't heavy because she'd been tricked into buzzing up a killer, Sam learned moments later. They were heavy because Logan's sister was pregnant.

Hugely so.

The woman's face, so like Logan's only packaged in a more delicate, feminine manner, brightened with a small smile that did little to lighten the obvious strain. "Surprise?"

"You shouldn't be here." Sam blocked the doorway with her body, not even sure she had the right. "Cage said you were safe on the base."

Hazel eyes a shade lighter than Logan's looked up at Sam, who was startled to realize she topped Logan's sister by a good four inches. "Cage doesn't know everything, and neither does Logan. I wanted to be here, in case..." She shrugged and moisture gathered in her eyes. "Just in case. They'll fly Stephen here for debriefing first. I want to be here the moment he arrives. So I'll wait." She tipped her head toward the rooms beyond Sam. "Can I come in? I've stayed here before, when Logan has been in between assignments. I was here just a few weeks ago."

Which explained how she'd known where to come. It also explained the questioning light in her eyes. She knew full well Sam hadn't been around a few weeks earlier.

She didn't move from her position in the doorway, as though letting Nancy into the apartment was an agreement that she should be there. But what was the alternative? Trehern's hired guns could have spotted her already. She could already be in danger.

Reluctantly, Sam moved back and ushered her inside. "There's something else going on. Something you may not know about." In fact, she'd bet her examining tables that Nancy had no idea how much danger Logan was in.

If she knew, she never would have come to visit. She would have known how much he worried about her.

"I figured as much. Logan seemed pretty stressed when I talked to him last." Nancy sank to the sofa with a grateful sigh. "So, tell me about it. And tell me about yourself, too. If I know my brother, it could be a while before he gets back."

Tell me about yourself. Sam suppressed a snort of hysterical laughter. What could she possibly say? *I'm a vet from a tiny beachside town. I don't like the city and I don't like fast-moving men with careers that take them away from home. After my last bad breakup, I vowed to find myself a good man, except that man just took up with my best friend back home.*

Oh yeah, and did I mention that someone's trying to kill me?

But Nancy's eyes begged for conversation. In that instant, Sam thought what it must be like for the other woman—traveling across the country, alone, pregnant, wanting to be with her brother while she waited for news of her husband's rescue.

Finding her brother not home. Worse, in danger.

And in the next instant, Sam thought she understood a

little of what Logan had said about not wanting to commit a woman he cared for to such a life. To such indecision.

Then she wondered where he got off making that call for someone else. Her temper spiked, buffered by the strain in the other woman's eyes.

Sam worried for Logan. Nancy worried for both her husband and her brother. Where did it end?

So they talked. Woman to woman for nearly an hour, about Sam's clinic and Logan's childhood, about Nancy's missing husband and her impending motherhood. But as they chatted, tension settled over the room.

Finally, a phone rang. Both women jumped and reached for their pockets. Sam's stomach clenched hard when she realized it was hers.

She pulled it out, flipped it open and locked eyes with Logan's sister when she said, "Hello?"

"Tell Logan to turn the volume up on his phone ringer," Cage's voice said, "I've tried him three times now. He damn well better not be ignoring me."

Sam's quick relief that it wasn't anything more dire faded to confusion. "Logan's not back yet."

A light sweat broke out across Sam's body, though she couldn't have said why.

"Yes, he is," Cage countered. "The global positioning on the signal from his HFH phone puts him in the building." Then his voice shifted to concerned. "The signal's been there for more than fifteen minutes. What do you mean he's not back yet?"

"He hasn't come upstairs," Sam said numbly. Oh, God.

What was wrong? Why was his phone in the building but not him? "His sister is here, though. She just arrived."

And hadn't seen Logan on the way up.

Cage cursed. "That's just what I need. Put her on the phone."

Sam handed the phone to Nancy, hearing only the pounding of blood in her ears.

Where was Logan? What had happened?

She reached for the doorknob and heard his voice in her mind. *Promise me you'll stay inside the apartment.*

She stepped outside, shut the door on Nancy's voice as she spoke to Cage, and called the elevator. Palms sweating, she pushed the button for the lobby. From there, she headed down farther to the garage. It was as though an unseen force pulled her there, to the place where William had held a gun on her and Logan not four hours earlier.

The garage was darker than before, as though the night outside had seeped through the cracks. Shadows reached for her, and the damp air smelled dead and wanting.

Sam shivered and reflexively rubbed her arms to soothe the goose bumps. She took a single step away from the relative safety of the elevator lobby doors and flinched when they slammed shut behind her.

She should have propped the door open. Logan had given her the key code, but the lock would slow her down if she needed to run.

Run, the walls seemed to whisper to her. *Run.*

She took another step away from the elevators, squinting at the hulking automotive shadows, trying to see one large enough to be the four-door pickup truck. "Logan? Logan, are you there?"

The walls threw her words back at her, but there was no response.

"Logan, damn it. Answer me!"

Nothing. Not even a groan.

Sam's stomach quivered. Maybe he wasn't here. Maybe he'd dropped the phone. Maybe…

Maybe she needed to be sure.

She walked toward the street entrance, away from the well-lit elevator lobby, toward the pools of encroaching shadow. She strained her ears and heard nothing, but then again, she hadn't heard Trehern's approach the last time.

She passed a VW Jetta, a rented Escort and a dark, hulking SUV. A car passed on the street outside, a man shouted.

Something scraped nearby.

Sam jolted and spun toward the noise but saw nothing. Heart pounding, she glanced wildly to the elevator lobby, which gleamed with far-away illumination. Safety. She took a running step in that direction…and saw Logan's pickup.

It was parked on the other side of the SUV, near the street entrance, in shadows so deep they leeched away the red color and left it gray.

"Logan?" She damned the noise and sprinted to the

truck, wanting him to be there, but at the same time hoping he wasn't. "Logan?"

She peered through the window and gasped.

A dark, man-sized shape lay across the bench seat, unmoving. She pressed closer and identified him by his jeans and shoes, though his upper body and head were obscured by the angle and the darkness.

"Can you hear me? Logan!" Panicked, she banged on the window. Her heart clutched when there was no response. No movement.

Nothing.

Off to one side, she heard a stealthy slide of movement. Or was that her imagination?

Focus. She needed to focus, though her pulse pounded in her ears. The truck doors were locked. Was there a set of keys upstairs? She didn't know, didn't care. She needed to get him out of there.

She scanned the cracked, stained cement floor looking for something, anything that would help. She dismissed a piece of tailpipe as being too light to do any damage, then saw that the cement pylon nearby was broken, as though someone had hit it with a sloppy parking job. Several fist-sized chunks of cement lay nearby.

"It'll have to do." The hairs on the back of her neck feathered to attention as she scrambled over and grabbed the largest chunk.

She stood and spun, half expecting to find someone behind her. But she was alone. At least for the moment.

Not stopping to think, she yanked off her light overblouse, wrapped it around her hand and slammed the cement against the driver's side window.

The impact sang up her arm and numbed her fingertips. The glass spiderwebbed, but didn't give.

There was no response from the unconscious figure sprawled limply across the bench seat. *Please let him be unconscious,* she prayed, nearly sick with nerves and the need to hurry. *Hurry!*

She drove her makeshift weapon into the window again, and this time it broke, showering the interior of the vehicle with chips of glass, though the bulk of it fell in as one fractured slab.

Heedless of her hands or arms, Sam reached inside, unlocked the door and yanked it open. "Logan!"

Her heart stopped.

He looked dead.

Chapter Nine

"Logan! Can you hear me? *Logan?*"

He registered Sam's voice first, and a spurt of relief nearly knocked him back under. She was alive. William hadn't gotten her.

He tried to reach for her.

Bad idea.

First, the pain hit. Then the rest of the memories came. William cold-cocking him in the shadows of an overpass. The sensation of being driven, the fear of not knowing where, not being conscious enough to ask, or to stop whatever would come next.

He tried to crack his eyes to see where they were. He saw only darkness, then a faint light when her silhouette shifted.

He groaned aloud. At the sound, she let out a rush of breath. "Thank God! Can you sit up? How badly are you hurt?"

Not badly at all, he discovered when he let her lever him up. His head hurt like hell, but even that receded after he took a few deep breaths. And there didn't seem to be any other injuries. He supposed he should be grateful to William for that, and for the fact that the enforcer had apparently only hit him hard enough the second time to put him out a few minutes.

He knew the right places to hit a man. He could have killed Logan twenty times over, yet he'd driven him back to the apartment complex and carefully locked him in the cab.

Why?

"Come on. Let's get you inside. I'm sure Cage is on his way, and I'll bet—" She broke off as she got a shoulder beneath his arm and helped him climb to his remarkably steady feet. "Never mind. You'll find out about her soon enough."

The tone of her voice told him there was a story behind the cryptic statement, but he didn't ask, because the words had triggered another memory, that of William's voice as he'd faded into unconsciousness.

You'll know I'm telling the truth soon enough.

But which truth? That Viggo hadn't ordered the shooters, or another truth? Damn it. Logan cursed under his breath as Sam helped him to the elevators. He didn't need the help, but a piece of him needed the human contact.

Hell, never mind the human contact, he needed the *Sam* contact. She was warm and soft and concerned, and though it normally made him uneasy and faintly guilty to know someone was worried about him, the faint crease between her eyebrows made him feel...

Cared for.

The thought brought an insidious warmth. He drew breath to speak, then heard a noise from the deep shadows behind the elevator shaft. His instincts shouted *danger!*

He pulled away from Sam and shoved her behind the shelter of his body, stronger now that William's pressure-point paralysis had fully worn off. "Who's there?"

There was no answer. But there was someone out there. He could feel it.

He herded Sam to the elevator. "Get those doors open. Hurry."

There was no further noise from the darkness, but he didn't breathe again until they were in the elevators, on their way up to the lobby. Then he rounded on Sam. "What the hell were you thinking? You promised to stay upstairs! Do you have any idea what could have happened to you in that garage?"

Her expression underwent an amazing transformation, from concerned to surprised, and from there to irked, and then downright annoyed. She shot out her chin. "Would you have preferred that I had stayed upstairs and you had bled to death?"

He loomed over her, stared down at her, tried to lose the warmth of caring amid the anger and didn't quite manage it. "I'm not bleeding. I was out for a few minutes, nothing more. I would have come to eventually and made it upstairs."

"And how were we supposed to know that? Cage said the phone GPS signal had been stationary for fifteen minutes!" She shouted the last word, then brushed past him to storm across the lobby.

He followed with a half wave to the security guard, who looked startled to see him. When the doors closed on them for the longer trip up to the penthouse, he crowded her with his body, though they could just as easily talk from opposite sides of the car. "Then you should have waited for him to come find me. What were you thinking?"

She stood on her tiptoes to get up in his face, eyebrows drawn together, eyes dark with an emotion he didn't dare name. "I was thinking that you were down there alone. Hurt. And I couldn't wait for Cage. I just couldn't. I had to know."

Sam's voice broke on the last word. Her eyes filled with tears that he had to believe came as much from exhaustion and stress as from worry for him.

Then again, he thought when her eyes darkened further and her breath hitched as though she had only just realized how close together they'd gotten, maybe the tears were for him, after all.

God knew his thoughts were all tangled around the image of her. What if she felt the same way?

The doors dinged merrily and slid open. They had arrived. He eased away from her, startled and not a little uncomfortable at the realization that two seconds longer in that elevator and he would have kissed her. Taken her. Loved her and not given a second thought to the consequences.

Until afterward, when there would be nothing but consequences for both of them.

"Come on," he said gruffly, turning away. "Let's call Cage. I've got something I need to—"

He froze just inside the penthouse.

"Logan! You're okay!" His sister lurched to her feet, her face reflecting shock, joy, relief and disbelief all at once.

"Nancy! What the hell are you doing here?"

His first thought was that it had gone all wrong with Stephen, that Cage had flown her in for the bad news. But there was neither devastation nor joy in her flushed face. Just quiet worry.

"Sam, I just got here. Where did you find him?" The question came from Cage, who looked similarly relieved.

"Downstairs in his truck," Sam answered, closing the penthouse door behind her. "He was unconscious. Locked in." A tremor on the last two words was Logan's only clue to what she must have felt on seeing him.

He reached for her. "Hey, it's okay. William knows how to put a man out for exactly as long as he needs him out." Including permanently.

She dodged his arm. "I didn't know that."

Of course she didn't, which was why she'd put her fist through his driver's side window in an effort to get to him. Vaguely remembering the crash and her curse, he ignored her efforts to push him away and gathered her close. "Let me see your arm."

"It's nothing."

At Cage's raised eyebrow, Logan said, "She put her

fist through the truck window to get to me." When he found a long, shallow slice along the soft skin of her forearm, he cursed. "We need to take care of this. You sit down and I'll go get my kit."

The scene reminded him eerily of just a few days earlier, when he'd sent her to her own bathroom to tend a bullet scrape. Only this time, he wasn't planning on letting her wave him aside with a quiet *it's fine.* He intended to be sure it was fine.

He turned to follow, and was brought up short by the sight of Cage and his sister.

And it struck him that he'd nearly forgotten Nancy was there. Sam had become his priority.

No, that wasn't right. He was simply paying attention to her because she was hurt. He hadn't chosen her over Nancy. He wouldn't.

But deep inside, part of him questioned that confidence.

Jerked back to the present situation, he said, "Stephen?"

Nancy shook her head, eyes filling, but it was Cage who answered, "Nothing yet. They've been delayed by weather. It could be another day or two before they can even go in."

Another day or two. God. He reached for her and hugged her tight, part fascinated, part frightened by the hard bump of her belly between them. Stephen's child. A little girl, the sonograms said.

God, Steve, you should be here, Logan thought fiercely, wishing he were in Tehru waiting out the weather, yet knowing he was needed here more.

"I'm sorry, Nance," he said into her hair, "But you can't stay here. I'm...I've got something going on right now. It's too dangerous. I can't wait with you."

"I know." She pushed away, her strength, as always, surprising him. "Cage explained everything. Although—" she poked him in the arm like she used to when they were kids and he was being a brat "—he wouldn't have had to if you'd been square with me." Her eyes darkened with worry, with censure. "You could have told me, you know. I would have stayed on base if I'd known about what was happening to you and Sam."

"I didn't want to worry you," he said as the words *you and Sam* shivered through him like a promise. Like a threat. He squeezed his sister's arm and stopped himself from touching her stomach, which he knew she hated, because she said even complete strangers thought it was okay to touch a pregnant woman's stomach. "You've got enough on your mind waiting for Steve to come home."

When he said it like that, it sounded like a foregone conclusion more than a far-fetched wish.

She snorted. "Idiot. Next time, tell me. It's my job to worry about you." She pulled away. "And since by the same token it's your job to worry about me, you can set your mind at ease. I'm going home with Cage. His place is as safe as this one, and unlike some people I've just met—and quite like, by the way—I'll stay put when I promise." She lifted a hand and touched his cheek. "Don't worry about me. Or when you do, because I know you can't help it, worry about Stephen for me. Don't worry for my safety—I'll be fine. Just keep yourself safe, and Samantha."

Logan caught her close, stuck between guilt and a bark of laughter that this brave, proud woman—almost a mother—had grown up from a rotten little girl who'd stolen his army guys and dressed them in lacy doll clothes right before all his friends arrived for an afternoon of play.

The two of them were polar opposites, he thought. Over time, she had grown better. He hadn't. The thought brought a renewed stab of guilt.

As though she read his mind, or perhaps his expression, Nancy frowned and poked him in the ribs, right at the ticklish spot few people knew about. "You're a good man, Logan, and heaven knows you've got more book smarts than me. But don't go thinking you can make decisions for Samantha the way you did for me when we were growing up."

Logan heard the words, but rejected the logic of them. "If I hadn't introduced you to Steve—"

"I would have met him on my own," she interrupted firmly. "Somehow." She pushed away, straightened her clothes and glanced at Cage, who waited discreetly in the elevator lobby. Then she touched Logan's arm. "Give her a chance to make up her own mind, okay?"

He held still for a moment, torn between the desire to take Sam for his own for however long it was possible, and the sure knowledge that it wasn't fair. She deserved better. Finally, he dropped his chin and muttered, "It's not that simple."

"Now you're getting it." Nancy flashed him a quick, impish grin that took fifteen years off her face, then immediately sobered. "Walk me out. Cage will want to know what happened tonight."

Logan kept his thorough report brief, knowing it would leave his boss as mystified as he was.

Sure enough, Cage frowned. "If Trehern has a contract out on you—and by extension, Sam—then why did William skip not one, but two opportunities to kill you?"

"He says there's no contract." Logan jammed his hands in his pockets and resisted the urge to check on Sam. She'd been in the bathroom too long, it seemed.

"Do you believe him?"

"I don't know. But he said…" Logan frowned, trying to remember William's exact words. "He said, 'You'll know I'm telling the truth soon enough.' Then he drove me home, locked me in my truck, and from what Sam said about hearing noises and feeling like there was someone else in the garage, I think he waited around to make sure I came to okay."

Or maybe he simply wanted to think that. He didn't know anymore. Fatigue pulsed from his temples all the way to his toes, and he felt an almost physical pull toward the apartment. Toward Sam. Toward the bedroom.

No. The two don't go together, his conscious mind argued. But other parts of him disagreed.

"I'll look into it," Cage promised, then looked toward the elevator, where Nancy awaited him. "And I'll keep Nance safe while we wait on word of Stephen. I promise."

He was one of the few men Logan would hold to a promise like that, one of the few he'd trust with family. And that was a lucky thing. With so many of the HFH personnel in Tehru, it was pretty much just the two of them.

"We'll talk in the morning," Logan agreed, and turned back toward the apartment, where Sam still hadn't emerged from the bathroom. Worry tickled the back of his brain.

"Hey." Cage waited until he turned back before asking, "Do you think it's possible the attacks weren't ordered by Trehern?"

Denial was almost knee-jerk. It had to be Trehern. Had to. But because Cage's expression demanded honesty, Logan shook his head. "I don't know anymore. But if it's not him, then who else?"

"You got any other enemies?"

Logan shook his head, having already been through the short list. "Nobody else who'd profit from having me out of the picture." At least he didn't think so.

"What about Sam?"

He snorted. "Come on. That's ridiculous." But when Cage didn't share the grin, Logan thought about it for a second. And sobered. The shots had been aimed at her front door. The brake lines on *her* truck cut, maybe at Bellamy Farms. He shoved his hands deeper in his pockets. "I don't know. She has an ex-husband and an old boyfriend. And her father was the Black Horse sheriff for a long time."

"Think someone might want to get back at him?"

The pattern of attacks shifted in Logan's mind, though didn't quite fit. "Maybe." He glanced toward the apartment. Heard a door open and shut. He turned toward the sound, needing to see her, to check the wound on her arm and make sure she was okay. "I'll ask her."

"Do that. And, Logan? Be gentle, okay? This has been a hell of a wild few days for a small-town vet."

It had been a stressful few days for a city-doctor-turned-operative, too, but Logan didn't voice the thought. He simply nodded. "Yeah. I know."

And he feared it would soon get wilder.

SAM STIFFENED when she heard the door close. Though she was in the kitchen area with her back to the door, she knew Logan had stayed behind when the others left. She sensed his energy pulsing through the connected rooms, felt his presence tingle along the nerves on the back of her neck and the sides of her arms, which were bared by the T-shirt she'd donned after her shower.

Goose bumps rose on her skin and she didn't bother to brush them away. It wouldn't have changed a thing.

The electricity would still be there.

"Sam."

She turned at the single, soft word and their eyes locked across the kitchen. Even though from the ten minutes she'd spent locked in the bathroom after tending the shallow scrape on her arm, she'd thought herself cried dry of fear and emotion, a new feeling surged through her now. Hot, liquid wanting.

Reaction, she told herself. Proximity. That was all it was, nothing more. The click of sexual chemistry she'd felt from the first, magnified by the shared danger, by the relief that he was alive. Unhurt.

She took a deep breath and meant to ask whether he'd like a post-midnight snack. But instead she heard herself say, "I thought you were dead. In the truck, I thought you were dead."

And the idea had hit her harder than she'd expected, harder than she'd wanted, just as the relief she'd felt when he first spoke had nearly washed her away.

It had been more than simple joy that another human being was alive, or that a friend hadn't been badly hurt.

No, it had been soul-deep release at the knowledge that he, Logan, was alive. That he was still around, that there was still time for them to make it work.

But make what work? Their relationship, like her others, was doomed from the start.

Yet she couldn't find it in her heart to care about the inevitable end. Not tonight.

"Sam, we need to talk." His expression was serious, his tone bordering on dire, but his eyes told a different story. Amber ringed with dark, they glowed with a nearly feral light as he moved farther into the kitchen, shrinking the space with his sheer presence.

Like hers, his body and emotions seemed to be telling a different story than his brain and voice.

He crowded her into the corner beside the refrigerator. The rounded edge of the cool marble counter pressed into her lower back and the warmth of his body seared her chest and belly. She licked her suddenly dry lips. "Talk about what?"

"William swears it's not Trehern after us." Logan glanced at her mouth, then back to her eyes.

The case. He was talking about the investigation. The danger. Not them. But as her conscious mind seized on the topic, her body continued to react to his nearness with a painful longing.

"Do…" She swallowed and forced the words through her tight throat. "Do you believe him?"

"I want to," he admitted, startling her with his honesty. "But I can't. Not after the things I've seen." He drew away an inch, as though the memories reminded him once again why he couldn't be close to her.

"And…?" she prompted, part of her wishing he would back off so they could have a rational, serious discussion, part of her wishing he would move closer so they wouldn't have to talk at all.

"And at the same time, he could be telling the truth. If he is…" He eased away a fraction more, just enough to give her room to breathe the air that seemed to have thickened and warmed in her lungs. "If he is, then we've got another problem."

It hit her then, slamming through the sensual fog to

leave her reeling. "If he's telling the truth, then we don't know who is after us, do we?"

Logan shook his head. His eyes reflected a potent mix of regret and want. "No. We don't."

"Who does Cage think it might be?"

"He wants me to ask you the same thing." As though realizing for the first time how close they'd gotten to each other—close enough to kiss, to love—he pulled away and strode to the opposite side of the room.

Chilled by his withdrawal, by the cool counter at her back that was slowly warming with her body heat, Sam folded her arms across her chest. Shock rattled through her, followed by denial and a spark of anger. The concept was incredible. Unbelievable. "He thinks *I'm* the target?"

Logan cursed. "Maybe. Possibly." He scrubbed a hand through his short brown hair, leaving it standing up in spikes. "Probably not, but we can't make assumptions. Not now." He took a breath. "What about your exes?"

Her stomach twisted, not because the memories were unpleasant, but because the whole situation sucked. This wasn't about her. It was about him and his job.

Wasn't it?

When he simply stood there, waiting for an answer, she cursed low and fisted her hands at her hips. "Are you asking for personal or professional reasons?"

She hadn't asked about his past relationships. For that matter, she hadn't asked about any present ones, though in the hour they had waited for Logan's return earlier that evening, Nancy had provided her with an unsolicited rundown of Logan's life from birth to present day. According to her, he'd had two somewhat serious relationships in college and medical school, and nothing since. The lack might have made her worry that he was commitment-phobic if she didn't already know.

He didn't avoid commitment for his own sake. He avoided it for the sake of the woman he might love. Right or wrong, he was stuck on the idea that it was unfair to ask her to love a man who might not come home from his next job, his next day at work.

Hell, Sam wasn't too keen on the idea, either. But that didn't seem to have stopped her from caring. Hadn't stopped her heart from breaking when she'd looked into that pickup-truck window and seen him motionless. Maybe not even breathing.

Personal or professional? Her question hung on the air between them, unanswered, a living thing that made her wonder. Want. His eyes pulsed molten at the centers, as though he felt the same. A ball of need gathered in her stomach.

And he turned away. "This isn't about us—it never was. If it hadn't been for those gunshots, we never would have spoken more than a passing word. We'd never be here." His gesture encompassed the city, the penthouse, the space that enclosed them together. Alone.

It shouldn't have felt like a rejection, but damn it, it did. Sam sucked in a breath and schooled herself not to show the hurt. This wasn't about sex, wasn't about love. It was about figuring out who had shot at them, who had cut the brake lines on her truck.

When she thought of it that way, it didn't seem quite as far-fetched to wonder if she had been the target all along. Except—

"What about the plastique in the refrigerator? That wasn't aimed at me. Not at all."

"True." He didn't relax his pose. "But that happened after the other two incidents, and might have been designed to get me out of the way so I couldn't interfere with the next attack on you."

Sam was chilled by the coolness of his tone, a stark contrast to the fire in his eyes, the air of tension that gathered around him. She shivered and held up a hand. "Okay. Point made. What do you want to know?"

"Would any of your exes want to hurt you?" He didn't look at her as he asked the question. A muscle pulsed at the corner of his jaw.

"No. Never." At his sidelong glance, she shrugged. "I pride myself on calm, rational breakups." Lord knew she'd had enough practice. "The relationships ran their courses, that was all."

"My parents have been married nearly forty years."

The faint hint of censure reminded her of her father's subtle disappointment. *Don't be like me, Sam,* he'd said. *Don't love the ones who don't want to stay.*

But then, like now, she hadn't been able to stop herself from wanting the impossible, from wanting a strong, adventurous man who would stay in a tiny beachside town where nothing much ever happened.

She met Logan's eyes and held them. "I married Travis right out of vet school. At the time, we were a perfect match. Both of us wanted small practices someplace quiet." She shrugged helplessly, a beat of sadness accompanying the memories of a sandy-haired student with wide shoulders and a go-getter's attitude. "By our third year, he was on the fast track to research greatness and I was learning how to palpate cows." That hadn't been the only problem between them, but it was the easiest to summarize. "The divorce was simple. Amicable."

"Where is he now?" Logan's expression was lighter now, as though he found no reason to suspect Travis.

Or, her stubborn heart interjected, *no reason to be jealous of him.*

Ignoring that as wishful thinking, she answered, "Cornell Vet. He and his wife are both instructors there. We keep in touch." In casually friendly letters once or twice a year. Sometimes less.

"And the other?"

She tightened her arms across her breasts and glanced down at the rich marble of the kitchen floor. "Same story. We met, we clicked…then we unclicked when he got tired of Black Horse." *Of me.* "We've stayed friends."

Distant friends, which made sense. If they'd had enough in common to stay good friends, they would have made their relationship work, wouldn't they? She had simply chosen the wrong man. Again.

Or so she told herself. It was easier and less painful than thinking maybe the lack was in her. To think that maybe she wasn't capable of the deep, strong emotions that hurt enough to cry for.

To kill for.

When Logan didn't respond, she shrugged and tried not to feel like a failure. "So the answer is no, neither of them would want to kill me."

His eyes bored into hers. "And your father? Would anyone want to use you to get to him?"

The twisted logic of it brought a shiver, but Sam held still, trapped in the intensity of his eyes. "I...I don't think so. You've seen Black Horse Beach—it's not a hotbed of criminal activity." At least it hadn't been until Logan had arrived. "The sheriff's job mostly involves riding herd on the tourists and dealing with DUIs. I don't remember my father ever being involved in anything really bad. Not something that would be worth killing over, anyway."

She looked at the floor, thinking, *What if he had been and didn't tell me?*

What if he'd put someone in jail and the parole board set the criminal free?

What if she'd been the target all along?

The thought was chilling. Terrifying. It had been bad enough thinking she was in danger because of her association with Logan. But to think that he was in danger because of her? That she was being personally stalked by killers?

The idea shouldn't have made it worse. But it did.

"Hey." Logan's voice startled her. She hadn't heard him move, but he was suddenly close enough to touch. His eyes were warm amber, the darkness hidden at the back now. He lifted a hand and traced a finger down her cheek, leaving shivers behind. "You're safe here. I won't let anything happen to you."

"And you? Who's going to protect you?" Her voice came out sharper than she'd intended, edged with nerves and his unsettling nearness. "When I saw you in the truck…" Her heart had stopped. Simply stopped. She bowed her head and found that her forehead rested comfortably on the slope of his chest. The position muffled her words when she said, "I thought you were dead."

"Hey," he said again, and nudged a finger beneath her chin to tip her head up. "I'm fine. You don't need to worry about me. It's my job to worry about you."

No, it's not, she wanted to say, *I can take care of myself.* But she said nothing, because she was trapped in his eyes, in the heat and flash of them. In the warmth of his body pouring into hers and the inevitable knowledge that he was going to kiss her. That this was all wrong.

And all right.

Then he kissed her, and she couldn't think anymore.

Chapter Ten

This was the king of all bad ideas, Logan knew, but he couldn't seem to stop himself from kissing her. Even as his brain fired every warning buzzer it owned, his body moved closer, his lips slid across hers, his tongue slipped between.

He'd intended the kiss to be a quick flyby, an affirmation of his vow to protect her, no matter where the danger was coming from. He'd intended—

Hell, who was he kidding? He just wanted to kiss her, bad idea or not. The more they'd stood in the kitchen together, voices saying one thing, bodies saying another, the more he'd wanted to kiss her.

And oh, so much more, though the more couldn't happen. Not tonight, not ever.

So he contented himself with a kiss. Or at least that was how it started.

The moment their lips touched, the moment she sighed into his mouth and returned his tongue's caress, all his intentions exploded in an enormous boom of light and color and sound, all bouncing around inside his skull and resolving themselves into a single sensation.

Heat.

ONE MOMENT SAM WAS CHILLED with fear, with uncertainty, and the next there were no remnants of winter in her body. She was July, August, blazing sun and sweat all concentrated into one single point. His mouth. On hers.

What am I doing? she thought, then realized she knew exactly what she was doing.

Taking what she wanted, damn the consequences.

She'd known it would come to this if they stayed together for any length of time. How could it not? The chemistry crackled between them like a live, greedy force. She couldn't deny it.

Didn't want to.

So when he angled his mouth across hers and sought entry with his tongue, she opened her mouth, opened her arms and yes, damn it, her heart, and let him in.

One night, she told herself, she'd give herself one night to feel safe, to feel the flame.

And then she'd walk away. She'd have to, or this could be the one to destroy her carefully constructed life. He wouldn't mean to. He wouldn't even see it, or he'd feel bad if he did.

But she'd be destroyed, nonetheless.

"Sam." He cupped her face between his warm palms and traced kisses along her ear. "This is probably a really bad idea."

His voice was ragged, his breathing fast, his heart keeping pace with hers.

"You're right, but I don't think I care right now." Her voice was unsteady, too, and she felt a flutter of panic when he crowded her with his body, wedging her deep within the corner formed by an L of marble countertop. But the panic quickly warmed to desire at the feel of him against her, the hard, throbbing planes of his chest and thighs, the maleness between. She gasped when he pressed against her. She pulled his T-shirt from his waistband and slid her hands beneath to touch hot male skin and hard muscles.

He flinched and hissed out a breath, his whole body tensing when she dragged her short fingernails across his ribs.

She smiled in wicked delight. "You're ticklish?"

"And I'll deny it to my dying breath."

The word *dying* shivered between them, more prophetic than joking, bringing images of dark garages and shoreside cliffs. She sobered. "I don't want you hurt because of me."

"Same goes." He framed her face in his hands. "We don't know which it is. The best thing we can do is stay here tonight, where we're safe. We can start making calls in the morning."

There, in the marble-trimmed kitchen, the danger seemed to press them close even as it pushed them apart. But at the same time, it seemed distant, locked outside the secure apartment complex.

Waiting for them.

"And until then?" Sam gripped the countertop at her back.

His molten eyes cooled a degree, grew wary. He withdrew a scant inch, so their bodies were less intimately aligned. "We should get some sleep."

The question was implicit in his tone. *Will you stay with me?*

Sam knew she shouldn't, but couldn't deny the want. The need. But though she wouldn't walk away from him unscathed, she vowed to go into this knowing she would walk away. He wasn't the sort who would stay, and he certainly wouldn't ask her to come with him.

He didn't want the responsibility. He'd made no claims otherwise. And though his solitary lifestyle worried his sister, she had summed it up in a line during their earlier conversation, *He doesn't want to leave anyone else behind.*

Well, Sam didn't intend to be left behind, not again. This time, she'd do the leaving.

Later. Once the danger was past. But for now…

For now, she wanted this. She wanted *him.*

Damn the inevitable consequences.

So she touched his hands where they still cupped her face and said, "Yeah, sleep sounds good," and stood up on her tiptoes to kiss him, letting her lips and tongue answer for her.

He groaned and his hands streaked down to fist at her waist. He bunched the fabric of her clingy top and drew it up, baring her stomach. Then he trailed his fingers across the soft skin there, the gentle touch at odds with the wicked play of his tongue, the heated press of his body.

Passion shimmered through Sam in electric currents of desire. She pressed closer, then gasped when he boosted her atop the counter and stepped into the natural V of her legs, which were hemmed in by the angle of the lower cabinets against her calves. The upper row of cabinets pressed against her shoulder blades and the back of her head.

She was trapped. Deliciously so.

Lust shivered through her, tempered with a thread of nerves as she was reminded how big Logan was. How strong. She knew he would never hurt her physically, but there was something sexy about her sudden realization that she was weak in comparison to him.

Yet still she had power. It was in his eyes when he pulled away and looked at her. "Are you sure? I'm not…" He took a breath and seemed to force the words. "The time with Trehern changed me into someone I don't even know anymore. Someone I'm not sure I like. Until I figure that out, I won't be good for anyone. I'm not sure I ever will be."

It hurt her that this was how he saw himself, that it was what he thought she saw. So she touched her lips to his in a gesture of healing that quickly warmed to more. Before they lost the thread entirely, she pulled back and said, "I'm not asking you for anything, Logan. I don't want promises or explanations. Our lives aren't just going in opposite directions, they're not even on the same train track. But this…" She slid a hand down his chest to rest above the button of his jeans and had the satisfaction of seeing his eyes go blank, then dark. "This is a place where we can meet. For tonight."

She said the words firmly, as much to convince herself as him.

"For tonight," he repeated, and she couldn't tell whether he was sealing the bargain or reminding himself.

Then she didn't bother to wonder anymore. She acted. Felt. Gloried in the slide of skin on skin. Reveled in his groan when she wrapped her legs around his waist and aligned them center to center. When she poured herself into a kiss.

He fisted his hands gently in her hair, swore reverently and bent her back to touch his lips to her breast through the clinging cloth. The shirt frustrated, inflamed, even as the denim barriers below both prevented completion and added torturous friction.

This was what she'd wanted, Sam thought as she let her head fall back and wallowed in greedy abandon while Logan drove her mad through her shirt. Beneath it. This was what she'd needed, to prove that she was alive, that he was alive.

That they were both safe for the moment.

The danger outside lent an edge of desperation to her actions and she scooted off the counter and dropped her feet to the floor. "Come on." She offered her hand. "Want to show me the bedroom?"

"No," he growled, startling her. But confusion was cleared the moment he tugged at the snap on her jeans, slid the zipper and tugged them down. "Here first."

Here, she thought with a naughty thrill. He wanted it there, in a brightly lit kitchen high above the city lights. High above the danger.

The wide windows and open floor plan gave her the feeling that anyone passing by could look in and see them. But who would be passing by the top floor of the high-rise? Seagulls. Maybe a helicopter. They were exposed, but private with it.

"Okay?" Hands on the button of his own jeans, Logan paused and cocked his head.

The faint chill of conditioned air bathed her now-bare legs. She should have felt ridiculous standing in a marble-and-brass kitchen with her jeans around her ankles, but she didn't. She felt sexy. Empowered.

Hot.

"Perfect." She smiled, toed off her shoes and socks, and stepped out of her jeans. Clad only in a clingy shirt and lace-edged panties, she reached for him, needing to touch the smooth, sculpted muscles that were being revealed to her bit by bit. "Let me."

The heat spiraled around them, building to a roar as they stripped each other naked and scattered clothes across the highly polished floor tile. The room should have felt cold, sterile, but the warm brown of the stone set off the wide sweep of his shoulders as he closed the scant distance between them and boosted her back onto the counter.

The marble cooled the skin of her buttocks and thighs even as the heat from his body seared her front.

A kitchen was no place for foreplay, she thought as she hooked her ankles behind his hips and fastened her lips to his. Bedrooms were for foreplay and soft sighs, for unions that would last beyond the night.

Kitchens were for flash and flame and the slap of flesh, which was exactly what he gave her.

"Sam." Her name was a raspy breath from his heaving lungs as he cupped her breasts and nipped at her chin. "What are we doing?"

She kissed him, and unintentionally poured a part of her soul into it. She felt the sharp tear in her chest, heard an almost audible rip, and closed her eyes against the power of it. The regret.

Keep it light, she told herself, and answered, "We're doing what we've both wanted to do for a month, since the first moment you knocked on the clinic door to pick up the key to the cottage."

If they'd acted on the impulse then, would things have happened differently?

His eyes flashed to molten amber. "If that's the case, then I should bend you over my arm—" he suited action to words "—and kiss you like this."

He touched his lips to hers and hot spikes of pleasure reared up to overwhelm her. Cool sizzles of contact existed beside searing bursts of want. Nerves coexisted with a feeling of safety. Danger with protection.

So like their relationship to date.

Then he groaned her name, and everything shifted to want. Need.

Fire.

They came together in a rush of straining limbs and heartbeats. He sheathed himself with a condom that must have come from his wallet and entered her with one sure stroke, almost before she was ready for it.

No, that wasn't quite true. Her body was well past ready. Her heart, however, hadn't been braced against that moment of joining. Of connection.

He filled her, stretched her almost to the point of pain that quickly blurred to edgy pleasure.

She opened her eyes—when had they fallen shut?—and was shocked to find the room so bright. Always before for her, intimacy had been cloaked in darkness and euphemisms.

But now she found herself trapped in Logan's eyes, in his complete and all-consuming awareness as he thrust into her, withdrew and thrust again. She saw the smooth curve of his shoulder, the taut lines of muscle across his chest and ribs, the surge of him into her body, the thrust into the center of her, which coiled hot and ready, her body far ahead of her mind.

With a shudder of shock and recognition, she thought, no, *this* was intimacy.

And as the spring of pleasure wound tighter and tighter still, as Logan drove into her with the power of a warrior and the gentleness of a lover, Sam fought to close her eyes and retreat back into that safe, dark place.

But she couldn't. She was trapped in his wanting expression as though he'd reached into her body and cupped her heart. She couldn't read his emotions, she could only feel her own. Passion. Excitement. Fear.

And when his eyes blurred and he shouted her name, when the tension whipped tight within her then sprang free and radiated outward, she felt the strongest emotion of them all.

Completion.

The feeling rioted through her, caught the aftershocks and perpetuated them until her whole body hummed with the orgasm and the moment.

When she returned to herself, minutes later, or maybe an hour, she found him watching her steadily. His chest rose and fell rhythmically, pressing them together and flexing the place where they were still joined.

"Regrets?" he said quietly, his eyes betraying nothing.

"No," she answered automatically, defensively. Then she took a moment to look inside and discovered it was true. There was fear, yes, and a beat of sadness that she couldn't even hope to hold on to this feeling, this man. But there were no regrets. Not yet. So she shook her head, smiled and softly said, "No regrets."

A fine quiver ran through his body and he exhaled. "Good." He backed away from her, slid out of her, his magnificent body etched in exquisite detail by the harsh overhead lighting. "Come with me?"

She put her hand in his and they walked into the bedroom together. He went into the bathroom to dispose of the condom and came out with a handful more, bringing a smile to her lips. And when he turned out the bedroom lights but left the bathroom lit to provide a soft, indirect light, she realized she'd been wrong all along.

Intimacy wasn't in the lighting. It was in the man.

THEY TURNED TO EACH OTHER twice more during the night, yet still managed to rest and recover from several hectic days.

The world intruded just shy of 6:00 a.m. when Logan's phone rang. He cursed and he reached for it, only to remember it was in the kitchen with his pants.

He and Sam had paused for food around three, but hadn't bothered with the clothes.

Sam. Though the phone continued its digital burble, he swung his feet to sit on the side of the mattress, and looked back at the bed. At Sam. The sight of her punched him right in the soul.

In sleep, the worries of the past few days had smoothed from her face. She looked younger and happier, yet at the same time more fragile, as though a careless word or touch might break her.

A twist of guilt accompanied the thought. Though they'd set the ground rules the night before, there had been something in her eyes, something in her touch that concerned him. Too much caring, perhaps. Not enough distance.

Or was that what he was feeling?

The phone fell silent and he flinched at the sudden quiet. Unable to force himself away from her, he reached out and traced a finger along the delicate skin of her cheek. When she was awake, her jaw was set with determination and a little bit of the devil. As she slept, it softened to a gentle line. A vulnerable curve.

The phone rang again and he froze. What the hell was he doing? This was a one-night thing. They'd agreed to that, hadn't they? A one-night thing that had stretched through until morning only because the penthouse was the safest place for them to be.

That thought brought the memory of William's voice at his ear, the shiver of not knowing whether he would live or die. Whether he had brought the danger straight to the woman he had promised to protect.

Suddenly filled with the need to be somewhere, any-where other than that bedroom, he snatched his hand away and stood quickly, heedless of his nudity. He followed the sound of the phone and grabbed it from beneath the breakfast bar.

He answered it as he pulled on his pants. "Hello?"

Half expecting it would be Nancy with good news or bad, he steeled for her voice and was surprised to hear Cage's deeper tones. "Logan, you'll want to come down to the Chinatown station."

A chill skittered through him. "What's wrong?"

"There's been a second sting in the Trehern organization."

Logan's confusion solidified to disbelief, then a

surge of excitement as Cage briefly sketched what had gone down.

"We'll be right there," Logan promised, then hung up on his boss.

He turned to find Sam in the kitchen doorway wearing a sheet and a worried expression. "What's happened?"

He paused a moment, once more struck by her beauty. The early morning sunlight glowed through the wide windows and gilded her golden hair. Her jaw was no longer a vulnerable curve, but rather a firm angle where it met her neck, just at the place where he'd discovered she was extra-sensitive to his kisses.

"Logan? Is it Nancy's husband?"

"No," he answered, a beat of disappointment managing to coexist with the excitement of what had happened overnight, while they slept. According to Cage, there had been no proof of Stephen's life. No break in the weather to allow the rescue team into the Tehruvian backcountry. The knowledge dimmed Logan's thrill when he said, "It's Trehern."

Sam swallowed convulsively and moved into the kitchen to gather her clothes, which were spread around in an abandon that had felt perfect the night before, but in the morning light seemed almost…inappropriate.

She pulled on her clothes before asking in a forcedly firm voice, "What about Trehern?"

Logan blew out a breath, still not sure he understood—or believed—everything that Cage had told him. "There was a federal sting last night on what was left of Viggo's operation, which was being led by his son, Viggo Jr. Apparently, they had planted more agents than just me and…Sharilee." It still hurt to say her name, but perhaps the pain had faded, just a bit. "There was a delivery out on the waterfront last night. Drugs. The feds—led by their undercover man, William—set out a net for the rest of Trehern's people and busted them good."

Logan felt a fierce joy that the bastard's reign was well and truly over, and baffled relief to learn that William was one of the good guys, but those emotions were tempered with…

Regret?

He glanced over at Sam, who hugged herself as though cold. Her face had grown pale. She said, "Then William must have been telling you the truth. And that means Trehern didn't send anyone after us."

"Not exactly." Logan snagged his shirt from the floor and pulled it over his head before saying, "According to Cage, one of Viggo Jr.'s men says he ordered the hit. He can identify the assassin." He shoved his hands in his pockets. "Once he's cut the deal he wants, we'll know the identity of the shooter. Who knows? The cops may already have the bastard in custody."

He should have been elated. But one look at Sam's pale face, one thump of his heart against his ribs told him he was anything but.

"So this is almost over?" she said quietly, neither her voice nor her expression giving anything away.

"Yeah. It's over." He turned away and headed for the

door. "Come on. Let's get going. We can grab some coffee on the way to the station."

But as the elevator doors closed on them, trapping them in thick, tense silence, one thought beat through Logan's brain with life-giving rhythm.

He didn't want it to be over. Not yet.

Chapter Eleven

Sam felt out of place at the Chinatown station as official-looking men and women rushed past her with official-looking files and scowls. But she couldn't have stayed behind in the penthouse and waited it out. She just couldn't.

It was over. Logan's words echoed in her brain, taking on new, deeper meanings every time she repeated them.

The danger was over.

Their time together was over.

She'd known it was coming. She just hadn't been prepared for it to come so soon. If she'd known, she might not have made love with him—for that was what it had been, love. Not sex, no matter how hard she'd tried to keep it that way.

"Sam? You want to hear this?" Without waiting for an answer, Logan took her elbow and steered her through the seething crowd of bodies.

"Is it always such a zoo here?" she asked in a desperate attempt to keep it casual, to hide her confusion over what had happened between them, what would happen next—and to avoid the inevitable answer, which was *nothing*.

"Not this early." He gestured her into a small, dim room, one wall of which was a slab of reflective-coated glass. "The last stages of this sting were a combined effort between the local cops and the feds, so they brought a bunch of the scum here for questioning. This is Martin Gross."

Sam stepped away from Logan and touched the glass. On the other side, a dark-haired man sat alone at a banged-up conference table. His features were regular and pleasant, his body fit enough beneath a dark silk shirt and darker slacks. But his expression was…unnerving. His eyes and mouth seemed salacious and vicious at the same time, a creepy combination of twisted sexual energy and murderous rage.

She shivered, backed away from the glass and bumped into Logan, her back to his front. The flare of warmth threatened to drive her into his arms, but her sense of self-preservation held her away.

Don't make this more difficult than it already is, she told herself firmly before she turned around and looked up into his eyes. "Who is he?"

"One of Viggo Jr.'s lieutenants. He claims he ordered the hit on me." Logan glanced past her to the room beyond, and his eyes hardened. "He gave the cops a name, an address. They should be bringing the bastard in any minute now, so I want you to stay in here. Just in case. It's safe."

A shiver crawled down Sam's back. How could she be unsafe in a police station? But she understood what he was saying. They wouldn't be safe until everything was certain.

Worse, tension gathered around Logan. A waiting, watchful edge.

She touched his arm. "What aren't you telling me?"

He glanced down at his arm, at her pale hand silhouetted against his tanned skin. His face held a blend of worry and regret. "William was hurt in the raid."

Since touching him was too much of a temptation, she withdrew her hand before she asked, "How badly?"

"They're not sure. He's at Boston General now." Logan muttered a curse and shoved his hands in his pockets. "He swore to me the hit hadn't been ordered by Trehern. Now we've got this guy claiming it was…." He strode to the opposite end of the small room, his restless energy bouncing off the walls and jangling her nerves. "It doesn't add up."

"Maybe he didn't know. Maybe they had started to suspect him and didn't tell him everything."

"Impossible. William's cover was flawless. That's why they left him under when they pulled the rest of us out." Logan turned toward her. His eyes reflected turmoil, indecision and something else. "So how could the hit have been planned without him knowing about it?"

She sensed that the question was rhetorical, doubted he'd even hear if she answered as he paced the room like a caged beast, seemingly more agitated than the situation demanded.

For a fleeting moment, she wondered whether he was upset about what had happened between them the night before, when a night of mutual desire had turned into something more. At least for her. So she stopped his next pass with a hand on his arm. "Logan, do you want to talk about it?"

He froze. His jaw worked as he swallowed, but he kept his eyes glued to the one-way glass. "About what?"

Did she imagine a note of reluctant hope in his voice? She took a breath to settle the nerves suddenly twisting in her stomach and said, "About last night. I know it got a little…intense. But I want you to know that I meant what I said. I'm not looking to start something serious with you. I'm country and you're city. I've learned from experience that the two don't mix."

But the pat explanation didn't ring as true as it once had. Though she'd been comfortable thinking her past relationships had failed because of geography and different levels of ambition, now she wondered if the love simply hadn't been strong enough.

Worse, what if *she* was the one who'd let the relationships fail? What if she had compromised more? Loved more? Could those relationships have worked?

More importantly, would she have wanted them to? Though she'd blamed their failure on her choice of lust over common sense, she hadn't felt half the burn with those men that she did with Logan, which made him a danger.

He stared down at her, eyes unreadable. "I agree completely. We wouldn't work."

But his voice was flat. His eyes didn't waver from hers.

She fidgeted, tugged at her shirt and tried not to remember him pulling it off her the night before. "Good. I'm glad we got that settled, then."

"Yeah, it's settled." He spun to the door and yanked it open. "Stay in here. I'll be back."

And he was gone, taking most of the restless, edgy energy with him. Some of the itchiness found its way to her, expanding in her chest until she had the ridiculous urge to cry. She closed her eyes tightly and willed the tears back.

This was the way it had to be.

She heard a door creak and opened her eyes on a burst of hope that Logan had come back to say no, he didn't want it to be over between them, damn it. But the noise had come from the room next door, where Martin Gross slouched at the scarred conference table. The sounds were transmitted to her room via an intercom that made them seem tinny and distant, though the men on the other side of the glass were only a step or two away.

"Martin." A middle-aged detective with a hang-jowled face that made him look rather like a fish sat down opposite the slouching man. "We've arrested Frankie on your say-so. Can you explain to me why he claims to have no idea what you're talking about?"

Gross's face twisted into something more vicious, less salacious. "Because he's a liar."

The cop—or fed, Sam wasn't sure who was who—sighed and leaned back in his chair. "Come on, Martin. Don't screw with me. A deal's not a deal unless you give me something real."

Gross snorted. "Hey man, that rhymed."

Watching from the other side of the glass, Sam couldn't believe that Martin Gross, nearly her age and normal looking aside from his expression, had hired someone to kill Logan.

It was unbelievable.

She shivered slightly and rubbed her arms, feeling terribly alone in the small room. In the police station. In the city.

Logan had been her support for the past few days, but he wasn't there. She'd sent him away and they'd agreed it was over. Done. Kaput.

God, she needed a friend.

Tears pressed as Sam pulled her phone from her pocket and the men continued to talk in the other room. She dialed a familiar number, needing the connection. The feeling of not being alone.

Jen answered on the first ring. "Black Horse Veterinary Clinic, may I help you?" There was no giggle in her voice this time, no gasping for breath, but her tone was lighter, happier than Sam had ever heard it.

Her heart lifted a bit. At least something good might come of the past few days.

"Jen, it's me," she said into the phone. "How are things there?" *How is Jimmy?* she wanted to ask, but felt a little strange doing so. Jimmy had always been *her* friend first. Now it was different. But in a good way. She'd get used to it.

Eventually.

"We're fine," Jen said dismissively, then her voice sharpened. "How are you? What's going on? Have they caught those men yet?"

"Yes." Sam glanced through the glass and saw Gross gesturing wildly as though trying to convince the other man of something. "It looks like they have."

"Ohmigod! I'm so relieved." Jen's whoosh of breath carried clearly on the airwaves. "When are you coming home?"

"Why?" Sam's heart picked up a beat and she deliberately shifted her thoughts back to Black Horse Beach. "I thought you said everything was fine."

"It is," Jen assured her, "but I can only do the small animal stuff—I'm no good with the cows and goats, never mind the horses. I've sent the emergencies up north, but your message board is filling up fast. Thomas Bellamy has become fast friends with your voice mail."

Normally that sort of news would have brought a faint sting of guilt and the warm peace of knowing she was needed. Knowing where she belonged.

Today, it brought a beat of sadness. She pictured her message board and the clinic, and for the first time in her life, the cheerful space seemed...

Small.

"I don't know when I'm coming back, Jen." Sam cracked the door to the hallway, thinking to find Logan and see where they stood. With the investigation. With each other.

Two men stood outside with shoulder holsters strapped over button-down shirts, deep in conversation.

"You think Frankie is guilty?" the older of the two asked.

"Seems like a lock to me. Gross is puking the information like there's no tomorrow."

"What about what Doc is saying, how William swore Trehern wasn't in on the hit?"

Sam paused in the process of closing the door, aware of Jen waiting on the line, and of the two men in the hall talking about Logan.

"I think Doc Hart is reaching. He was undercover for a long time, and it messed him up good. Besides, he has his sister to worry about right now—I heard the team went in after Steve an hour ago and hasn't been heard from since. Hart must be a mess, so he's going to have to leave this to us. We've got Frankie locked in. It's over."

Sam closed the door on that echo of her and Logan's earlier conversation. *It's over.*

She didn't need to be here. He didn't need her here— he needed to concentrate on Nancy now. So she lifted the phone and said to Jen, "I'll rent a car and be there in a few hours. You can forward any emergencies to this phone."

It was time to go home.

LOGAN SCOWLED AS HE WATCHED the feds question Frankie Donovan for the third time. The little weasel still maintained his innocence, which worried him.

Sure, Frankie was a liar, and a convincing one at that. It was part of the job description of a paid killer. But there was something…believable about his denials. Add that to William's assertion that Trehern hadn't ordered the hit, and the end result was a very bad feeling in the pit of Logan's stomach.

He cursed and turned away from the one-way glass, acknowledging that Frankie's supposed innocence wasn't the only reason he felt like hell.

Sam's easy dismissal had hurt more than it ought to. They'd agreed to keep it simple, damn it. Mutual satisfaction, no strings attached. So why was he pissed off that she'd stuck to the deal?

Maybe because that morning, as he'd touched her sleeping face, he'd started to think about strings. About commitments. About trying to find a way they could keep seeing each other after this was over.

But that was impossible, as she'd reminded him. She was committed to her town and her life. Who was he to mess with that? Worse, who was he to come in and put her through the same bad times she'd already been through?

He couldn't promise to stay, and he couldn't promise to come back. Sharilee's death had shown him the truth of that, as had Stephen's abduction. That the rescue attempt seemed to have gone awry only served to reinforce what Logan already knew.

Love should be about being together, not about worrying.

"I swear to God, man!" Frankie's voice rose to a frustrated shout. "Gross never hired us to kill Doc. If he says so, he's lying."

Clearly, one of them was lying, but which one?

A tingle of instinct told Logan the answer wasn't the one he wanted. He turned for the door, intending to check on Sam, and froze when it swung open.

William stood in the gap wearing a sling over a T-shirt and jeans that were at odds with the natty suits and silk shirts Logan had always seen him in.

Undercover. The truth of it still rattled him, as did a flash of anger. Though he hadn't meant to ask, he blurted, "Why didn't you help Sharilee?"

The other man's eyes blanked as though he'd expected the question, as though the memory didn't hurt him.

Or maybe hurt too much.

"You were there," William said quietly. "You know there wasn't time. Wasn't warning. Viggo just… freaked." He snapped his fingers in a lonely emphasis that echoed in the small room, counterpointed by Frankie's continued attempts to make the interrogator believe his version of the story. "And afterward, what would you have had me do? The first sting took out Viggo Sr. and his top three, but you didn't get Viggo Jr., and you didn't get Gross and the others. There was enough manpower for them to rebuild the whole damned organization from the ground up. So tell me, what should I have done?"

The quiet question knocked Logan back a step, as did the expression of quiet anguish in the other man's eyes. "We should have saved Sharilee. Somehow."

"We couldn't have. Not the way it went down." William took a step farther into the room. "It wasn't your fault, Logan. It wasn't mine. Trehern would have murdered her whether we stepped forward or not, except if we stepped forward he'd have killed us, too, without missing a beat. And you know what? The organization would still be going strong. We did the right thing."

The truth of it pulsed through Logan like pain, washing away a fraction of the guilt, though none of the sorrow and loss. "The right thing sucks."

"Yeah, it does." The men traded wary looks, not quite friends but no longer enemies. Then William glanced through the one-way window. "What's he doing here?"

"Martin Gross claims Viggo Jr. took out the hit on me and Sam without telling you. He says Frankie was the shooter."

William bit out a curse. "That's bull, and anyone who doesn't know it is an idiot. It was all over the organization that HFH was looking for names, trying to figure out who was after you two. Gross is just trying to cut a phony deal and save his own ass."

A chill settled in Logan's gut. "Are you sure?"

"Positive." William turned to him. "Think about it.

If you're Viggo Jr. and you've just been handed the reins to your father's organization, what's the last thing you're going to do?"

The awful obviousness of it hit him. "He wanted me to testify against his father. He wanted the old man in jail so he could run the organization." Oh hell. Logan swallowed and said with grim certainty, "*He didn't hire the hit.*"

William nodded. "Precisely. I guarantee you that Frankie will come up with an alibi, or else Gross will trip himself up. He's spinning a story to save his own hide, nothing more."

"Then who the· hell is after me? Or are they after her?" Logan cursed. This knocked off one set of suspects and opened up a world of others.

"She have enemies?"·

Logan thought of Sam and damned the clench in his gut. "Her father is a retired sheriff. Someone might be trying to get to him through her."

William flicked off the intercom, cutting off Frankie in mid-whine. "What about her? What does she do? Anything there?"

"I don't think so. She's a vet, strictly small-town stuff, cats and dogs, tourists and stuff. The only mega money in the area is a racehorse farm, and they've got their own vet. Territorial sort."

The other man's eyes sharpened. "How territorial?"

·"I don't know, but it doesn't feel right. Then there's this other guy, a real snake. He fights dogs outside of town, near the dump." Logan pictured Horace Mann and felt a twist of dislike. "If she has an enemy, it's him. He might be just crazy enough to take a shotgun to her if she interrupted one of his fights and tried to lock things down. But premeditated murder? I don't see it." He jerked his head toward the door. "Let's go ask her. She's watching Detective Sturgeon question Martin Gross."

Except when they opened the door to the small room where he'd left her, Sam wasn't inside.

"Doc?"

Logan turned at the hail. Officer Drews held out a folded sheet of paper. "She asked me to give this to you."

On an oath Logan unfolded it and scanned the two short lines, then crumpled the paper in a rage of hurt and worry.

"Where is she?" William said.

"She's gone home." Logan jammed the paper into his pocket and spun for the door, yanking his cell out as he ran. "She thinks she's safe, that we've got the killers. She has no idea." He punched in the clinic number she'd given him when he first rented the cottage. When the Black Horse sheriff answered, he barked, "Jimmy, Sam is on her way home, but she's still in danger. Give me her cell number." He jotted it down on the fly. "Okay, if you see her before I do, keep her safe, okay? Just keep her safe."

He was only half aware of William following him to the truck and jumping into the passenger's side. At his glance, the other man shrugged and said, "We couldn't save Sharilee."

The inference was clear. Maybe they could save Sam. Maybe.

Logan nodded curtly and cursed when his fingers fumbled the key in the ignition. "Strap yourself in. And here—" He tossed the phone number over. "Call her. Tell her to find someplace to wait. Someplace public where she'll be safe."

He started the engine and pulled out into traffic, ignoring the bleat of horns and a quick squeal of tires in his hurry to get to Sam.

To save her.

"Voice mail," William reported tonelessly, then left a quick message for Sam to call them. He disconnected and turned to Logan. "Maybe she doesn't have a signal."

Or maybe she'd already been taken. Cold air whipped in through the broken window and the icy fear drove Logan faster down the highway. William braced his feet to keep from banging his injured shoulder as Logan weaved through traffic like a madman, driven by one pounding thought.

He had to reach her in time.

Had to.

SAM HAD ALMOST REACHED the turnoff for Black Horse Beach when her cell rang, surprising her. This stretch of highway was notorious for bad signal strength.

She flipped it open. "Hello?"

"Dr. Blackwell? Thank God I've caught you! The people at your clinic said you were on your way back.

We need you here right away!" The unfamiliar voice was rushed and breathless, though lacked the tears she associated with most veterinary emergencies.

"Who is this? What's wrong?" Adrenaline surged through her, clearing away the useless regrets and second guesses that had plagued her drive. Logan needed to concentrate on the Trehern trial, and on his sister. Period. There was no room in his life right then for anything else. He'd made that clear enough.

"This is the manager at Bellamy Farms. You've gotta come quick, I've got a colt here who's cut himself up bad. He's gonna bleed out if he doesn't get some help."

Bellamy! Sam drew a breath. "Where is Dr. Sears?"

"Gone. I don't know where and I can't reach him. You've gotta come, Dr. Blackwell. Please?"

She could be at the farm in ten minutes. And even though she resented how they'd ordered her off the property only days before, it wasn't the horse's fault people were idiots. Arterial bleeds were serious. Fatal. The colt needed help now, not later.

Her internal debate was over almost before it began. Of course she'd go. But there was one problem.

"I'm in a rental car and I don't have any of my instruments with me." In fact, most of them had been in the truck and were now ruined. "I'll have to run to the clinic first and pick up my injectables and some sutures."

She could cobble together a large-animal kit from the spares in the back room. Let the feds have what was in the truck. Hopefully they'd be able to tie the sabotage to Trehern's goons and nail them for a good, long time.

That thought inevitably brought Logan to mind—his gentle, soothing touches the night before, and the hot, inciting ones.

The farm manager's panicked response broke through her foolish sensory flash. "We don't have time for that! Just come straight here and you can use Dr. Sears's equipment."

"He'd be furious," she said, while inwardly acknowledging it was the best option.

"Rumor has it he won't be working here for long." The barn manager's voice turned pleading. "You come right now and I'll put in a good word for you with Bellamy, I swear it."

She would have gone for the sake of the horse alone. But the possibility that Bellamy was thinking about replacing his staff vet decided her. She took the next turn, onto the winding road that led to the farm. "I'm on my way. But when Sears wants my head for touching his equipment, remember that you suggested it."

Her blood surged, as it always did when she was headed for an emergency, maybe a little more this time because the fates had handed her another opportunity with Bellamy.

"Will do." The barn manager disconnected with a click and she folded her phone so she could drive with both hands.

She spun the rental around a tight corner, glad to

think about her work, about the goals she'd had before Logan Hart's arrival in Black Horse Beach.

Before the night they'd spent together in the city.

She sighed as a remembered heat worked its way through her body and her mind replayed bright kitchen lights, brown marble and the tense, taut line of a masculine shoulder in Technicolor glory.

She sent the car around a slow curve between two small tangles of forest.

Pop!

The rental car jolted and dragged into the wrong lane. Damn it, she'd blown a tire!

Sam felt a second jolt and slammed on the brakes, heart jackrabbiting.

What the hell was going on?

The passenger-side window imploded with a crash. She screamed and yanked on the steering wheel. The car spun in a complete arc and stopped dead, blocking both lanes.

She stared dumbly at the missing window, then at the dark figure just visible at the edge of the woods. Tree-dappled sunlight glinted off the barrel of a rifle.

The shooter!

Sam screamed. Ducked.

And the bastard shot out her windshield.

Chapter Twelve

"Leave her alone!" Sick with rage and fear, Logan floored the gas and sent the pickup hurtling toward the shadowy armed figure.

The gunman cut and ran straight back into the trees.

"I've got him!" William jumped from the truck and bolted into the forest. "You check on the woman."

The woman, Logan thought. *Sam!* He was out of the truck between one of his thundering heartbeats and the next, sprinting to the rental car.

As he ran, the fear pounded in his bloodstream. If he'd been five minutes later, he would have gone straight to the clinic. He wouldn't have seen her turn off the road. Wouldn't have followed her.

Wouldn't have been in time.

But was he? What if he was too late after all?

He reached the car, yanked the driver's side door open—

And saw Sam huddled in the foot well. Alive.

The rush of relief nearly brought him to his knees.

He didn't think twice about reaching down, pulling her into his arms and hanging on tight as his heart threatened to bang through his rib cage and out for her to see.

"Are you okay?" he asked as she shook in his embrace. "Damn it, Sam, are you hurt?"

"I'm okay." She clung for a moment, then pushed away. "He didn't hit me." She rubbed her hands up and down her arms, seeming not to care that she brushed away small chips of safety glass.

Logan shoved his fists in his pockets as panic shifted to anger in a heartbeat. She was okay.

But she might not have been. He could just as easily have opened the door to find her slumped across the front seat, a neat hole in her forehead, the back of her head blown away.

"Why did you leave the station?" He'd meant to ask the question reasonably, but it came out in a muted roar. "What the hell were you thinking?"

She could have been killed. Logically, she should have been. They'd gotten lucky.

Her fingers flexed on her arms. Crossed in front of her chest, they formed a shield, a flimsy barrier that might shut him out but would never stop a bullet. "The shooter was captured up in the city, wasn't he?" Her voice climbed toward the breaking point. "Then who was that? Who the hell was that?"

Brush crashed nearby and Logan spun, putting himself between Sam and the tree line, then relaxing when he saw the light-colored flash of a hospital sling and

William's familiar deadly walk. The fed was covered with wet leaves and a powdering of pine needles. He looked disgusted. Tired. In pain.

"You lose him?" Logan asked.

"Yeah. Bastard was fast, and I'll bet you a hundred he's local. Knew exactly where the path was to get down this slippery hillside. By the time I got to the bottom—mostly head over heels—he was long gone."

Sam looked from one man to the other, eyes dark with confusion, arms gripping each other spasmodically. "What's going on here?" She glanced at William. "I get that you're not on Trehern's team, but what are you doing here? What are either of you doing here? And who just shot at me? I thought you people had the assassin in custody!"

Sensing incipient hysteria, Logan took a step toward her, then stopped when she backed away. He reined in his emotions when he wanted to shout because she looked like she might shatter. The fragility he'd seen that morning as she slept had come to the forefront, though she wouldn't thank him for mentioning it.

He spread his hands, aware of William keeping watch at his back. They needed to get her to shelter. To safety.

It was seeming more likely by the moment that she'd been the target all along.

"We thought we had them, but we didn't. Martin Gross was lying. Trehern never hired anyone to go after me."

Her mind made the connection instantly and her eyes flashed with panic. "Then they're after *me?*"

He took a step toward her, the need to get her into the truck thrumming through his veins. "We don't know that." Though it seemed likely—and unlikely at the same time.

Why would anyone want to kill Sam?

As though reading his mind, she shook her head. "I'm the town vet! Why kill the town vet?"

"I don't know." He was close enough to touch her now. He linked his fingers around her arm and drew her close, though she held herself stiff. "But we're going to find out."

"I led them right back here, back to my town. My friends." There was a quiver in her voice now. Half a heartbeat later, she flinched and said, "No. I didn't lead them back, did I? They were waiting for me. They've been here all along."

He didn't bother to deny it. How could he?

"Logan, we need to move her someplace safe." William's quiet statement sent a shiver through Sam's body and Logan held her closer.

Someplace safe. But where?

"Come on." Logan gestured her to the truck, which leaned drunkenly where he'd left it halfway up a hill. The three climbed into the vehicle in a tense, watchful silence. The forest seemed to have grown eyes and ears. It watched.

Waited.

Logan gritted his teeth as he boosted her into the cab, fired the engine and aimed the truck back toward the road.

He never again wanted to experience the terror he'd felt when he'd seen the gunman fire into the windshield of her rented car. Was that what Nancy had felt when he'd gone undercover? What she felt when she waved Stephen off on his next assignment, or when she'd heard he wasn't coming home?

God, it was an awful feeling. If that was what it was like to care about someone in danger, he was doubly determined to spare Sam the agony.

Though he hadn't managed to spare himself.

Hands locked on the steering wheel, Logan stopped the truck at the verge of the road, turning neither toward nor away from Black Horse Beach.

He cared about her. The realization streaked through him like a threat. A promise. He might be able to keep Sam from caring about him, but he'd apparently failed miserably at not caring for her.

That's what the emotion had been as he'd driven toward the gunman. Panic laced with caring. He hadn't needed to rescue her because she was in trouble, or because he was making up for not having saved Sharilee.

He'd needed to save her because he couldn't imagine a world without her. Couldn't imagine *his* world without her.

He needed her.

Oh, hell.

"We going?" William's voice asked from the other side of Sam. The men had automatically sat on opposite ends of the bench seat, flanking her. Protecting her.

Logan glanced over at the rental car. Two flat tires, a broken passenger-side window and shot-out windshield left it looking like the victim of a nasty, private war.

Which is exactly what it was, except they had no idea what enemy they were fighting against.

"We should go back to the city," he said aloud. "She'll be safe in the apartment." He wasn't sure why he even bothered to voice the thought. It was the obvious answer. The right one.

And he knew she would hate it.

Sure enough, she snapped back, "No way. This is my town. My home. I'm not letting them drive me out, not again." She glanced from Logan to William and back. "And besides, they didn't follow me to the city last time, so they probably won't again. I'm not leaving my friends in danger when my presence could very well draw the shooters out into the open long enough for you and the cops to catch them."

That, Logan realized, was the reason for his hesitation. The strategist in him wanted to drive her to the clinic and stake the place out until the bastards showed their faces.

The man in him wanted to lock her away in the highrise where nobody could touch her except him.

He was aware of William's implacable gaze, of the other man waiting for him to make the call.

As though aware of his dilemma, his turmoil, Sam touched his arm. "Please, Logan. Think of how I'd feel if Jen or Jimmy were hurt because of me."

Think of how I'd feel if you were hurt, he wanted to shout, but understood her point. Worry and obligation weren't a man's prerogative, he thought, and was surprised to realize he'd wanted them to be.

"You want to go to the clinic?" he asked, though the answer was obvious.

She withdrew her hand, and the place where she'd touched felt cool in comparison. "I trust you to keep me safe."

"Okay, then. The clinic it is." He spun the wheel and aimed the truck for Black Horse Beach.

He just hoped her trust wasn't placed wrong.

Dead wrong.

HALF AN HOUR LATER, Sam's head spun as she sat behind her desk in the vet clinic. She put down the phone with a final-sounding clunk. "They didn't have a colt hurt, and Dr. Sears won't be leaving for his conference until tomorrow morning."

Logan made a noise in the back of his throat that sounded caught between a snort and a growl, stood and strode to the far side of the waiting room.

She dropped her forehead to her hands because she didn't want to watch him pace, didn't want to admire the clean elegance of his stride, didn't want to imagine the sleek play of muscles beneath his clothes—images made so much more vital by the events of the night before.

True to her vow, she'd walked away. More accurately, she'd run without saying goodbye, without checking to be sure that the suspects in custody were the true shooters.

Stupid. She'd been stupid on so many levels. And now she was back where she had started, except that everything was different.

She glanced at Logan and amended, *she* was different. She'd been changed by knowing him, and where would that leave her when he left?

Miserable.

"Bellamy's farm manager didn't make the call, did he?" Jimmy asked quietly, surprising Sam, who'd all but forgotten the others were present.

William slouched near the door, body angled toward the street, gun within easy reach. He formed a picture of casual deadliness that gave her a serious shiver.

Jimmy and Jen sat close together on the waiting room bench, not touching, but not far away either. Good. Jen deserved a steady, dependable man. One who wouldn't ask her for more than she could give or give her less than she deserved.

Well, hell, Sam thought, *so do I.* Too bad she wasn't attracted to that sort. No, she gravitated to the love 'em and leave 'em men. The dangerous ones.

The protective he-men who were so damned good at waving goodbye.

She glanced over at Logan and was instantly caught in his eyes. She read frustration there. Danger, and a hint of something softer she couldn't quite define.

"Sam?" Jimmy prompted, "was it the farm manager?"

"No," she said. "Bellamy's people didn't call me."

"So." Logan paced back and forth, hands jammed in his pockets and a scowl furrowed across his brow. "The call was a fake designed to lure you to that particular stretch of road. But how the heck did they know you were back in town?"

"I told them," Jen said quietly. She looked at Sam, guilt splashed across her face. "You said to refer emergencies to your cell phone because everything was all right and you were on your way home. I know how much you want Bellamy's business, so…" She trailed off and dropped her hand beside her chair, where Maverick stood guard. Now allowed the run of the clinic, the stray had adopted Jen as his human.

"It's not your fault," Sam jumped in quickly. "You were doing what I'd asked. How were we supposed to know the police hadn't caught the real shooter?"

She realized her mistake just before Logan's roar nearly shook the Victorian that housed her clinic. "You were supposed to stay in the police station until everything was clear! You were supposed to wait for me to come back and—" His teeth clicked shut, biting off whatever he'd been about to say. He glared at her across the room as though they were alone, and a tremble of fear—or perhaps excitement—worked its way through her soul.

Even now, even knowing how much it would hurt in the end, she wanted to be with him. To touch him, taste him. To store up the memories for when he was gone.

Jimmy's phone rang, shattering the suddenly tense silence. He answered and traded a few brief words with the caller before snapping the phone shut. "Nothing doing on the list Sheriff Bob gave us."

Before calling Bellamy, Sam had called her father, who had given her a brief list of the men he'd put into Walpole or one of the other area corrections facilities. Then he'd threatened to hop on the first plane out of Arizona. She'd only managed to forestall that by promising everything was under control, then handing the phone off to Jimmy, who was Bob's second favorite person in the world, Sam being the first.

It would have pleased him to see the two of them together, Sam knew. But the glow binding Jimmy and Jen together eased her heart, and made her think something good might come out of this mess, after all.

Then she glanced toward Logan, and knew something painful would come, as well. Because when he left—and he would—he'd take a part of her along for the ride.

But the rest of her would stay in Black Horse where she belonged.

"None of Sheriff Bob's old cases have recently been paroled? Damn." Logan scowled harder. "So what does that leave us?"

"Not much." William stretched his legs out and recrossed them at the ankles, managing to look casual and battle-ready at the same moment, even though he was exhausted and wearing a now-dirty sling. "It means we're either looking for an enemy Sam has made personally, or we're back to looking at you." He gestured to Logan. "You sure Trehern's the only one who might go after you? What about one of his competitors? Maybe someone out there would rather do business with Viggo Sr. and figured that with you out of the way, he'd walk."

"No. It doesn't feel right." Logan paused in his pacing, only a foot or so from Sam's chair. She felt the buzz of his nearness and caught a faint hint of his essential, masculine scent. The combination revved her body even as she fought to quell the reaction. This was a council of war, not a love affair.

She would do well to keep that in mind.

"Yeah." William exhaled. "I know what you mean." He glanced over at Sam. "So what's the plan?"

"I've been thinking about it." Logan abruptly dropped into the chair beside her and she nearly jumped away. His leg pressed against hers, and they touched at shoulder and hip as though joined together. "And as far as I can tell, Sam has only one real enemy in town, right?"

"Horace Mann," Jimmy said quietly, then nodded, though he still looked skeptical. "True, but I don't know if I see it. He's mean enough and crazy enough to kill, I'd say, but why bother? What benefit does he get from killing either of you? We've never come close to nailing him on the dogfighting, and even if we do, what then? He gets a fine, maybe a few months in jail…." He shook his head. "It doesn't really play for me."

"You got another suspect?" Logan challenged, body tensing, though he didn't stand to pace again.

"The caller seemed to know an awful lot about Bellamy. He knew exactly what to say to get Sam over there…." Jimmy trailed off, eyes sharpening as he thought. "What about Dr. Sears?"

Sam jolted. "The farm manager said they were thinking about firing him. No, wait." She paused, trying to mentally align the players. "It wasn't the farm manager on the phone, was it? It was someone else."

"It was the shooter, or someone involved with the setup," Logan agreed. "But that's a good point. The rumor isn't common knowledge, is it? If we can confirm that Bellamy is thinking about firing his regular vet, then we know two things. One, the caller knows the farm, and two, Sears has a motive. He's trying to protect his territory."

William looked unconvinced. "Is that really a motive, do you think? Surely he could find another job."

"Not like this one," Sam argued. "Bellamy is the biggest thing in the area—heck, in the country. You've seen the sign…they have the highest winning percentage of any other racing stable on the planet. Until earlier this spring, they stood a very successful, very expensive stallion at stud. He died a few months ago, so they'll lose that income, but his last foal crop is dropping now. Those babies are worth millions. The vet that cares for them…" She gestured helplessly. "Suffice it to say, Sears makes a mid-six-figure salary and has a luxurious house on the estate. He's not likely to give that up without a fight."

But would he kill for it? The very idea was chilling. This was a *vet* they were talking about. Someone like her.

"I'm still not convinced," William said, "but it sounds like it's worth checking out." He glanced back to Logan. "Plan?"

Logan sighed. Sam felt the swell of his ribs against hers, the press of his warm flesh and tried to suppress the flash of heat, the slide of security, which she knew was only an illusion. "I think Jimmy should check out Bellamy. He's official, so should be able to get on the property. We need to know whether Sears's job is in jeopardy." He stood, paced to the window and said with his back to the group, "I'm going to pay Mann a visit."

"And the rest of us?" William asked quietly.

Logan glanced down at the man he'd wanted to call friend and now could. "Whether you want to admit it or not, you're about to drop. You and your bad shoulder are staying here. I need you to protect the women."

Sam stood and fisted her hands at her sides. "I'm going with you to Horace's place." She lifted a hand to forestall his quick protest. "I know the property better than you, and I not only know where he keeps the dogs, I can drug them if necessary. You need me."

The last came out huskier than she'd intended, almost wanting, and she cleared her throat against the sudden tightness as Logan spun to face her.

But instead of the automatic denial she'd expected, she saw reluctant acceptance. He scowled. "I don't like it."

She chanced a step forward. "But you know I'm right." She glanced at William. "He'll keep Jen safe. Him and Maverick. As for me, I'll trust you to keep me safe." And she'd do her damnedest to protect him in turn. "Okay?"

He glared, but didn't object. Their eyes held for a heartbeat before he turned away. "Fine. We leave in half an hour. Be ready."

Sam nearly shivered at the ring of deadly portent in his words, and at the spontaneous growl that echoed from beneath Jen's chair.

Even Maverick thought this plan could use some work. But what choice did they have? Either they went after the killers, or the killers would come after them.

After *her*.

Logan eased up on the gas after they turned off the main road toward Mann's place and tried to ignore the strain in his soul. He hated bringing Sam with him, but they hadn't been able to hammer out a better idea.

No matter how they'd looked at it, Sam was right. He needed her.

But damn, he didn't like it one bit. There were too many things that could go wrong, too many ways she could be hurt.

Or worse.

She touched his arm. "I'll be careful."

He glanced over and saw the nerves in her eyes, off-set by the dark clothing she'd chosen, hoping to blend in to the dim, gray light. The weather had turned stormy and night had fallen sooner than he'd expected, which was both a blessing and a curse.

A blessing because it might camouflage their search. A curse because they might not see approaching danger.

Bad idea! his mind warned. This was a bad idea no matter how he looked at it, but what was the alternative? They couldn't very well fortify the clinic and wait for the next strike.

No, it was better to attack, to search the premises for evidence, for a connection.

Any sort of a connection.

"Down there." She indicated a narrow, overgrown path.

"It's a fire access road that'll put us almost directly behind Mann's place. Kill the headlights, though, just in case. If there's a fight tonight, he'll have lookouts posted."

The idea of a dogfight hadn't even occurred to Logan, and he cursed himself for the lapse. There would be too much commotion, too many bodies around, most of them probably drunk or armed, or both.

He should bail on this now. But he didn't. He killed the headlights and turned onto the dirt path she'd indicated. The truck bumped and shuddered, leaves and branches slapped the windows and roof, and the gloaming light gave the whole scene an eerie, surreal feel.

"Here," she said softly, as though she, too, was affected by the creepy scene. Then again, why shouldn't she be? This sort of thing wasn't in her job description the way it was in his:

He stopped the truck and killed the engine. He briefly debated whether the quick getaway of a running vehicle was worth the possibility that someone might stumble on the truck and drive off, then pocketed the keys. Feeling as though he was stalling, he turned to Sam. "You don't have to do this, you know. You could wait here for me."

Instead of the tough-girl snarl he half expected, she gave him a brave smile. "I've got the control stick to manage the dogs with, remember, and the tranquilizers just in case."

He saw nerves behind her smile and was obscurely relieved. If she was afraid, she'd be careful. She'd listen to him. They'd be okay.

So he nodded, held a finger to his lips to caution silence from here on in, and slipped from the truck as she did the same on the other side. They walked through the woods single file, ears straining for a noise, eyes for a hint of movement, but everything was quiet.

At the edge of the tree line, he paused. Her gentle touch on his arm directed his attention to the barn, where two dozen cars and trucks were parked in haphazard order.

Oh, hell.

She leaned up on tiptoes to get her mouth close to his ear and breathed, "They're fighting all right. Bastards."

A cheer rose from the barn, which was a hulking black shadow against the dusk. The bloodlust in the sound was barely diluted by distance. As they watched, a late-model BMW pulled in and parked. A man's silhouette emerged and headed for the barn.

Logan had always imagined dogfighting to be a sport for ill-educated, violent men. But the class of vehicles below suggested that evil appealed to all kinds.

"They're occupied right now," she whispered in his ear, the warmth and breath sending shivers through him, heat fighting the darkness down below. "We can get into the house and look around without anyone being the wiser. Horace lives alone and he's sure to be in the barn. Or—" her voice sharpened with excitement "—we could call Jimmy. With a fight in progress, we'll have all the evidence we need for an official warrant."

"Call Jimmy," he said on a wash of relief. "Let's not be stupid."

Without warning, the muzzle of a weapon pressed into the skin below his ear.

"Good idea," said an unfamiliar voice. "Don't be stupid. Put your hands up and don't make any sudden movements. Feel free to yell for help, though. Nobody's going to hear you."

Shock blasted through Logan and he tensed to spin and fight, but a quick glance over at Sam showed a shadowy figure behind her, a gun at her temple.

Logan froze. How had he missed seeing the sentries?

How had they snuck up on him? He cursed even as his mind raced and he sought a means of escape, an opportunity to turn and fight.

His captor, big and rough, shoved him down the hill. "Let's go."

"Where are you taking us?" Sam's voice seemed unnaturally loud.

The man behind them chuckled grimly. "To the match, of course. You've been jonesing to come to one of our fights for quite some time, haven't you, Dr. Blackwell?" The weapon nudged Logan forward. "Well, consider this a personal invitation."

Logan growled and turned his head toward Sam. Their eyes locked and his anger surged when he read her fear.

But through the fear, she said, "You're going to let us watch a dogfight?"

Her voice was still too loud, making Logan wonder whether she'd seen someone in the trees, someone who might come to their aid. Then even that thought was washed away by his captor's next words.

"Not watch, darling." They stumbled down the hill, toward the dark-windowed barn. "You're going straight into the pit. There's nothing like a little fresh meat to liven things up."

Chapter Thirteen

Sam's captor breathed hotly against her shoulder and pressed moist lips to her neck. She gagged and struggled to free herself, but he had her control stick banded across her throat, pressing hard enough to subdue and panic, not hard enough to choke.

She glanced over at Logan and saw from his locked jaw and cold eyes that he was planning something—a foolish, violent counterattack that could get them both killed. Or both liberated.

Do it fast! she urged inwardly as they were force-marched toward Mann's barn. She dragged her feet and stumbled to slow them down, but the gun at her back and the cruel grip on her hair left little room for escape.

"Open up!" Logan's captor called. "We've caught ourselves some trespassers!"

A heavy curtain was drawn aside, revealing how Mann had kept the barn doors cloaked in darkness when the inside was lit bright as day. A cheer spilled out with the slice of yellow light, carrying the sounds of bets made and lost.

And over it all, the vicious, bloodthirsty barks and growls of dogs that had been bred to fight, then goaded beyond their civilized urges with hunger, drugs and taunts.

In an instant, the energy around them shifted from fear to action.

"Sam, run!" Logan shoved her aside, nearly breaking her captor's grip, and grabbed for the man behind him.

Heart pounding, she yanked free and bolted for the woods. She yelled into her fist, "Jimmy, I'm at Mann's. Get here as quick as you can!"

Something grabbed her ankle and she went down on her face with a scream.

The cell phone she'd hidden in her palm flung free.

"The sheriff's not here, babe. He's not going to save you, and neither is your boyfriend." Rough hands dragged her up off the ground and spun her back to the barn. "He can't even save himself."

She heard Logan bellow a foul curse, saw him swing a trained kick at the ring of men now surrounding him. Sam recognized a few as locals or residents of the nearby towns. Others were strangers. She took a step toward them and felt something tug at her ankle. She looked down and saw a long, thin pole with a retractable cable loop at the end.

She'd been caught with her own control stick.

"Ironic, don't you think?" the voice at her ear asked in a puff of hot breath and a heavy heartbeat.

Her captor freed her from the stick and used it to prod

her back toward the barn. Logan caught sight of them and the anguish on his face was almost painful to see.

Suddenly, Sam understood. He'd stayed behind to slow the others down. He'd meant to sacrifice himself for her.

The men moved in the moment his concentration broke. They kicked him, punched him, drove him to the ground and followed him down.

"Stop! You're killing him!" Sam cried, knowing it was no use, since murder was their intention. Her stomach knotted with fear, with pain, with a fierce need to stop the beating and the powerlessness of being unable to do so.

Then a figure stepped forward so he was silhouetted against the yellow light spilling from between the curtains. There was little human noise over the snarls and barks from within, as though each man—and a few women— had leaned forward to hear their leader's decision.

"Stop." The single word froze Logan's attackers, who quickly backed off as Horace Mann swaggered into the center of their circle and glanced down at the nearly unconscious man on the ground. "Bring him inside."

"What about the woman?" Sam's captor called, shifting his grip from her hair to her shoulder in an almost-caress.

Mann's eyes flicked to her and a small, cruel smile curved his lips. "Bring her, too. She can even have her little stick back…in a minute."

"You got it." Hot Breath shoved Sam forward, into

the barn. They passed through the light-blocking curtain and into another world, one of madness and blood.

The barn was the size of a four-car garage, and just as open. Bodies jammed the space, men and women, all slightly glassy-eyed with bloodlust. A series of cages lined one wall, each containing a dog.

But these were no tame house pets—not anymore, if they'd ever been. Crossbreds, they had the blunt, square heads of their pit-bull ancestors, but their shaggy, mottled coats spoke of other kin, as though Mann and his cronies had taken a pinch of every potentially vicious breed and mixed them into a stew of violence. Then they'd trained them to kill, shot them full of hormones and caged them to await the next fight. The next round of betting.

"Like what you see?" Hot Breath whispered in her ear. "You're going to get up close and personal in a moment."

He pushed her toward the center of the room. She was aware of men dragging Logan behind her, aware of his rasping breath and the pain radiating from him. The panic.

Or maybe the panic was hers.

The crowd shifted to reveal the pit. Twenty feet square, it was lined with waist-high plywood set in a metal frame. Blood darkened the cheap wood to mahogany. More plywood lined the bottom of the pit, to protect the floorboards from picking up evidence. Scattered sand played the same role.

No wonder she'd never been able to find anything in the barn before. Mann had a system.

Hot Breath released her suddenly and she spun, thinking to flee, to fight, to do anything to delay what might come next. She froze when Mann blocked her path. Looming. Armed.

"Dr. Blackwell." His mouth tipped up at one corner, though his eyes showed none of the smile. "I want to thank you for making my job so much easier than it's been for the past few days. You've proven harder to kill than I'd expected. At least until tonight." He gestured to his men. "Throw them both in, then bring me Diablo and Hades."

Hard, grasping hands pushed Sam to the pit, shoved her up and over the waist-high plywood wall. She heard a masculine curse, then Logan fell beside her. Instantly, his eyes opened, his body tensed and she realized he'd been playing more hurt than he actually was.

"You ready to get out of here?" he asked in a low growl.

Relief poured through her, leaving her weak and trembling for half a second before she pushed the feeling aside, knowing now was not the time. She could panic later, once they were out of there. She bowed her head close to his, as though checking his split lip and the redness beside his eye that would probably bruise if it had enough time. "What's the plan?"

"You still got those tranquilizers?" His eyes connected with hers and he lifted a hand to her cheek. To the crowd gathered around the pit, she imagined it looked like he was weakly grasping for help. But within the pit, she felt his gentle touch, saw the fire in his eyes and felt a measure of safety wash through her.

"You want me to tranq the dog?"

"No, I'll take care of the dog. You hit Mann."

She swallowed hard. "You got it."

Outside the pit, harsh male voices shouted, "Back off! Get back!"

Strong-backed men wearing heavy, elbow-length leather gloves pushed two of the cages toward the pit. They heaved a section of plywood up out of the metal frame and shoved the cages close, so the moment the fronts were slid upward, the dogs could charge into the pit.

Knowing it, the creatures pressed against the bars, snarling and snapping, slavering with the need to get into the pit. To attack. To kill. They seemed equally intent on each other and the humans.

To their drug-maddened brains, death was death. Blood was blood.

"Help me up." At his request, Sam pulled Logan to his feet and noticed he hadn't escaped the beating as unscathed as she'd thought. Blood stained his left leg and he favored his left side as though guarding cracked ribs.

The crowd shifted and boiled, the noise level increasing with each of Sam's rapid heartbeats. At first, she thought maybe Mann's devotees had come to their senses, that they were drawing the line at seeing humans fight the dogs in some sort of twisted, gladiatorial combat.

Then she realized it wasn't denial she was hearing. It was a renewed spate of wagering.

She set her jaw and turned on Mann, who stood at the end of the ring nearest the curtained barn doors. "You're even sicker than I've always thought."

"Compliments won't get you anywhere, Dr. Blackwell," he said with a mocking smile. In a casual gesture, he tossed her the control stick. "Let's see how well you use this in a real fight."

She caught the stick on the fly. She'd never before realized how flimsy the damn thing was.

"Sam."

Logan's urgent call spun her around just as Mann gestured grandly and said, "Release the dogs."

Willing hands yanked the doors up. The mottled beasts, one black, one a grayish-blue merle, leaped forward, then stood, quivering. Huge growls resonated in their chests as they ignored each other to focus on the humans.

"Get behind me," Logan ordered, "and be ready to hit Mann with that tranq."

Sam adjusted suddenly sweaty palms on the stick. "Do you want the control rod?"

He kept his eyes fixed on the dogs. "No. You keep it. Or better yet, drop it. Be ready to move on the count of three. One, two—"

The dogs lunged on two and a half. The crowd roared its approval. Men and women leaned close to the ring, shouting and screaming, their eyes glazed with bloodlust and fury. Sam's brain took a horrible snapshot of the image.

Then there wasn't time to think. Only to react.

Logan rushed the black dog and kicked it in the snout. The creature squealed and fell back, then came at him again.

Sam made a lucky grab with the control stick and managed to slide the cable loop over the merle's head. She yanked it tight, hoping to cut off the animal's wind, but the dog was too strong for her. With a snarl, it sat back on its haunches and ripped the stick out of her hand.

The dog shook itself, trying to rid itself of the stick, and succeeded only in swinging it from side to side, creating another hazard for her and Logan.

"Look out!" she screamed when the black dog made a running grab for Logan's hand.

The flailing control stick cracked the black dog across the face and it turned on the blue merle with a snarl.

"The tranq!" he yelled. Then he turned his back on both dogs, leaving himself horribly vulnerable. But the animals fought each other for a few seconds, snapping and growling, drawing first blood.

Sam yanked two of the single-use injectables out of her pocket. She'd brought six, but must have lost the others outside. Two would be enough to bring down Mann, she thought.

They'd have to be.

But once Mann was out, how did Logan expect them to get through the others? There had to be a hundred bodies crammed into the barn. There was no way out, unless—

Logan grabbed one of the plywood sheets. His face contorted with the agony of what must be cracked or broken ribs, and he ripped the wood from the metal frame.

Leaving the pit with a gaping hole at the end nearest the door.

Screams erupted and the bettors nearest the curtained door bolted for the exit. The noise and motion alerted the dogs, who stopped snapping at each other and zeroed in on the opening in the pit wall.

Freedom.

The black dog lunged for the gap and charged into the crowd, biting and snarling and seeming to revel in the panic as people scrambled over each other to get away.

Not all of them made it.

The blue merle set his sights on Logan, as he stood to heave the broken plywood into the crowd.

"Don't you dare!" Sam grabbed the dangling control stick and hauled onto it with all her strength. With it, she redirected the merle toward the gap and shoved it into the crowd.

Then she let go.

The merle cleared a path almost straight to Mann, who stood frozen in horror as his grand fight went to hell around him. Sam followed nearly on the dog's heels. At the sight of the approaching dog, or maybe the sight of her, Mann broke. He spun and ran for the exit.

The merle bit him in the calf and he went down. Sam landed beside him on her knees, grabbed the pole and shoved the merle away, into the crowd. The dog caught sight of the other caged animals, snarled and lunged in that direction, dragging the pole with him.

Sam jabbed the single injectors into the muscle of Mann's shoulder, one after the other.

"Bitch!" Mann rolled over, grabbed her by the throat and scissored his legs around her. His grip abruptly cut off her breath.

How long would the tranq take? Sam kicked and flailed wildly as feet pounded around her and human screams and canine snarls ripped through the air.

As she slid toward unconsciousness, she thought she heard her name.

"Let go of her, you bastard!" And then Logan was there, glorious in his rage. He ripped Mann's fingers from her throat and pulled her away from the rapidly failing dogfighter.

A white blur flashed past, snarling, and Sam was dimly aware that the other dogs were loose, wreaking havoc on the crowd still trapped within the barn. She heard shouts from outside, abnormally loud shouts that were distorted as though they'd come from a bullhorn.

"Jimmy's here!" she gasped, wincing when the words stung her throat. At Logan's sharp look, she said, "Just before they grabbed us, I'd speed-dialed him. The line was open."

His expression cleared, then colored with approval. "That's why you were talking so loud back there."

A vicious snarl brought them whipping around. The black dog stood not six feet away. Its throat vibrated with a horrible growl and its lips rippled back to reveal filed-sharp canines stained pink with blood.

"When I say the word, you run." Logan's quiet command brought fear and denial to Sam's throat, but she didn't have time to argue before he shoved her and shouted, *"Run!"*

She stumbled aside, a scream building in her chest. The black dog dodged Logan's kick, reared up and leaped for his throat.

A yellow blur passed between them, knocking the black dog aside.

Maverick.

It wasn't until Sam saw him face off against the black dog that she realized the truth. Even his plastered leg and stitched ear couldn't disguise the stray's resemblance to the black fighting dog.

Maverick hadn't been hit by a car. He'd been one of Mann's rejects.

When the black dog feinted toward Sam, Maverick snarled and charged. Perhaps he was listening to his bone-deep instincts to kill, or to the call of the blood-stained pit. Perhaps he was defending the woman who'd spoken kindly to him and scratched behind his ear.

Whatever the reason, he lit into the black dog and drove the creature away from Sam and Logan just as a human voice split the air.

"Freeze! Police!" At the shout, the light-blocking curtain was ripped down and bodies poured into the barn. Sam recognized the local deputies, along with some of the staties who'd come down to help with the truck sabotage and the cottage bombing. Armed, they fanned out and quickly subdued the twenty or thirty people still inside the barn.

Silence reigned with almost brutal quickness.

A lone dog remained caged. The others were gone, and Sam winced to think of the job she and Jimmy were going to have tracking them down. But the dogs couldn't be left loose. It wasn't fair to the animals, or the local pets.

Though the humans were the criminals here, the animals they'd taught to kill would lose out, in the end.

Then Jimmy was there, facing Sam and Logan across the motionless body of Horace Mann.

"He dead?" The sheriff nudged Mann's motionless form with a toe.

"He'll live," Sam replied. "But it'll take him the rest of the night to sleep it off." She stepped away from Logan's half embrace and wrapped her arms across her chest. "It was him, Jimmy. He tried to kill me." *He nearly succeeded.*

She shivered, then shivered again when Logan put his arm around her. She wanted so much to lean on him, to let him comfort her.

Then, like a flash of acceptance, or maybe resignation, she thought, *Why not lean? Why not take what you want?* It wouldn't be forever, or even for a while, but it would be for the night, and maybe that would be enough.

It would have to be enough.

So when Jimmy moved away to speak with one of the state investigators, she glanced up at Logan. "When we're cleared to leave, I'd like you to come back to the clinic with me."

His eyes sharpened on hers. "Well, it only makes sense. The cottage is going to need some redecorating."

But the tightening of his fingers on her flesh let her know he understood and was wholly in favor of her idea.

They deserved one last night together before they said goodbye. And if the ending was easier for him than her, Sam thought, it was her own fault for breaking her vow to avoid dangerous men.

For all that Logan was one of the good guys, he was the most dangerous sort of all. The sort she could fall for.

In fact, she feared she already had.

IT WAS FULL NIGHT before things wound down at Mann's barn, before the last of the bettors were shipped off to county lockup and the E.R. docs confirmed that Mann would live, albeit with a hell of a hangover from the canine tranquilizer Sam had sent into his bloodstream.

The bastard deserved that and worse, Logan thought, and locked his teeth against the rage. But the anger and the upset roiled in his stomach just the same, along with self-recrimination. If he hadn't brought Sam along to Mann's place, if he'd turned back the moment they saw there was a fight underway, if he'd…

If.

But he hadn't. He'd charged ahead and put her in

danger, exactly where he'd sworn not to put her. She'd nearly been killed, probably would have been if it hadn't been for her quick thinking with the cell phone.

He hated to think of her hurt. Couldn't think of the other option, the more permanent one.

"I'm fine." Her touch startled him, as did her words and the calm connection when she took his hand. "Jimmy says we can go now. The dogs they've caught so far will go to the county animal control office for treatment. He's taking Maverick back to Jen, and William is on his way to the city for the trial."

Logan was rattled to realize he'd forgotten all about the Trehern trial. It was set to resume the next day, and he was scheduled to take the stand.

But Sam seemed all too aware of it. She gripped his hand tighter. "You can drive back in the morning. You should rest those ribs."

The paramedics had poked the sore spots hard enough to assure themselves—and Logan, who'd been a doctor longer than either of them had been riding in ambulances—that he was bruised, not broken. But the injuries still hurt like hell.

However, he didn't think that was Sam's main motivation. He sensed a quiet desperation around her, as though she were grasping at one last night for them before he went back to the city.

He almost told her he'd come back to visit, but what was the point? He wasn't in this for the long term.

Aren't you?

He flinched at the pointed mental question that seemed to come in his sister's voice, but Sam left him no opportunity to consider what it meant. She tugged at his hand, leading him toward the truck, which was still concealed on the fire access road. "Come on. We can go home—go back to the clinic now," she corrected herself, reminding him that he'd been right the first time.

The clinic was her home, not his.

But when he opened his mouth to tell her this, she silenced him with a kiss that burned its way to his toes and brought all the roaring adrenaline back to fight mode. To explosion mode.

"Hush," she said. "It doesn't matter."

But he knew that on some level, it did matter. He just couldn't find the words, or the truth. Not yet.

She reached up and tugged him down for another kiss. The flames roared up between them, their tawdry surroundings faded to background, along with his aches and pains. He leaned into her, opened his mouth to her tongue and surged into her kiss, proving to himself that she was alive. They were both alive.

The danger was past.

That last thought set a small hint of warning bell through his mind, but that was obliterated in the next moment, when she slid her lips across his jaw to his ear, where she whispered a hot, naughty promise.

And he was lost. Whatever needed to be said between them—and he didn't yet know what that might be—could be said in the morning.

Tonight was for them. For their bodies. For being alive.

They stumbled to the truck together and collapsed across the bench seat in a tangle of arms and legs and clothing. Lack of a condom drove them to the clinic and upstairs to her bedroom where a pile waited in a little-used drawer.

There, in the light provided by a cut-glass lamp, he undressed her, following each motion, each piece of clothing with his mouth and hands until they both panted with need, with certainty.

They fell back on the bed together, and he was unsure where he left off and she began until the moment he reared above her, poised for the joining they both so desperately desired.

Then he knew exactly who he was. Who she was.

And who they were together.

He thrust into her on a cry and they rose together on a tide of passion that poured over them, tumbled them together and robbed them of breath as though they'd been too long beneath the waves. But it didn't matter. Breathing was unimportant as they clung together and rode the thundering crest down to completion.

And back up again.

And again.

SOME TIME LATER, when dawn stained the sky with pink glory, he felt the mattress dip and shift, and he reached for her.

"Go back to sleep." She touched her lips to his bare

shoulder. "I'm going to check on the animals, and maybe watch the sun rise. I'll wake you before you need to leave."

His sleepy, sated brain grasped that he needed to return to the city, needed to testify against Trehern, and then...

Then what? He didn't know, but he was quite certain the answer wasn't exactly what it had been a week earlier. Something fundamental had changed.

He knew who he was. Perhaps he wasn't the same person he'd been before going undercover, and he certainly wasn't the brash young doctor who'd risen to the assistant directorship at BoGen, then become bored with the position. He was someone else now. Older, and he hoped wiser.

Wise enough to make the right decision now?

He sure as hell hoped so.

It was with that thought, and with the imprint of Sam's lips on his shoulder that Logan fell back asleep.

The phone woke him some time later.

He was wide awake with a doctor's reflexes, out of the bed and scrambling amid the fallen clothes for the unit before he was quite aware he'd moved. He snapped it open before his brain fully processed the yellow light of morning or the fact that the other side of the bed remained empty. "Hello?"

"Where's Sam?" Jimmy barked.

"Downstairs feeding the animals," Logan answered automatically, though that had been hours ago. His instincts flared to life at the dire tone in the sheriff's voice. "Why? What's wrong?"

"Horace Mann finally came around and he's talking like there's no tomorrow."

Logan paused in the act of pulling on his pants and shirt, sudden foreboding icing his heart. "So?"

"He says it wasn't his idea to kill Sam. He was willing enough to do it, because he hates her guts, but it wasn't a rash decision. He was paid."

Jimmy hadn't even finished naming the villain before Logan hit the stairs. He charged down into the clinic and froze.

She wasn't there.

He scanned the note and lifted the phone to his suddenly numb lips. "She's on her way to the farm. Meet me there."

He tore outside to the truck without waiting for an answer, praying only that he'd be in time.

If he wasn't, Sam was dead.

Chapter Fourteen

Sam hadn't stopped to think, hadn't stopped to listen to the little voice that said, *This is what got you in trouble the last time.*

She'd been desperate to get away from the clinic before Logan awoke, before he climbed into his red pickup truck and waved as he pulled out of the driveway headed for the city. He might be kind and say he would come back. He might even visit once or twice, but she knew full well the goodbye was inevitable.

So she'd taken the coward's way out and bailed before the goodbye. She'd been halfway out the door to Jen's house, where she'd planned to drown her sorrows in chocolate-chip pancakes, when the clinic phone had rung. Not the cell. The land line her clients used.

Now she was on the road headed toward a narrow spit of land that shoved itself into the Atlantic, surrounded by water on three sides. The phone call had been Bellamy. Not the farm manager. Not a stud groom. Not a muffled stranger. It had been Thomas Bellamy himself. The owner.

"I want to talk to you about replacing Sears as my on-staff vet," he'd said, and she'd closed her eyes against a burst of relief, muted excitement and fatalism.

If she signed herself on as Bellamy's head vet, she would have no time for trips into the city. She'd need to be on-site as much as possible.

In a way, it might be a good thing, because it would remove any temptation to attempt a long-distance relationship, such as it was, with Logan. Even if he were open to such a thing, which she was pretty sure he wouldn't be.

He was too committed to being alone, to protecting the people around him from worry and pain. But he didn't seem to realize that the people who cared about him would worry regardless and pushing them away only caused more pain.

So she'd agreed to meet with Bellamy at the farm.

But as she drove out there in the little hatchback she kept at the clinic for use when she didn't want to drive the vet's van, Sam had second thoughts.

Then third ones.

"I've done this all wrong," she muttered aloud, realizing for the first time that she didn't have any right to resent Logan for not offering to stay, not offering to try a relationship when she'd never once told him she wanted him to stay. She'd been letting him off easy by not asking him to make the choice.

Honestly, she'd been letting herself off easy by not offering the choice. If there wasn't a choice, she couldn't be hurt by his decision.

Worse, she hadn't asked herself to make a choice, either. Would it be so awful for her to leave Black Horse Beach and make a start somewhere else?

For the first time in her life, the answer was *maybe not.*

Stunned, she turned between the stone columns that marked the main entrance to Bellamy Farms.

What had changed?

She was different, she realized. She and Logan together were different. But could it work?

There was only one way to find out. And that would involve turning down Bellamy's offer.

She climbed out of the truck and walked to the guard shack. This time, she was waved through without question. "Mr. Bellamy is expecting you," the young man said. "He'll meet you down in the broodmare barn."

Her feet followed the clamshell path while her mind spun furiously. Should she take the job and stay in Black Horse? Should she turn it down and ask Logan to take her with him? Should she play the middle ground and ask Bellamy for time to think over his offer?

God, she didn't know. Things that had seemed so simple, so black-and-white suddenly held new shades of gray.

New complications.

"Mr. Bellamy?" she called when she reached the wide, arching doors of the mare barn.

There was no answer, which seemed odd. Even this early in the morning, there should be stable hands feeding and mucking, grooms checking their charges.

She felt a shiver of unease, but passed it off as a by-product of the past few days as she stepped inside the barn. Her feet carried her to the third stall on the right, which held the pretty chestnut mare she'd helped birth a foal earlier that week.

When she reached the stall, her lips pursed in a silent whistle. The baby had seemed big when she'd helped turn him right way round and aided the mare in the delivery. Now, he seemed huge.

"You're going to be a monster," she said aloud, and admired the colt's straight legs, wide-set intelligent eyes and upright neck. "Classy looking, but a monster." She glanced at the clipboard hung neatly on the stall door.

And paused.

She looked back at the mare, suddenly putting her finger on something that had bothered her the other night, but had since been overridden by the danger…and Logan.

But now she pursed her lips consideringly. This was a thoroughbred racing stable. According to the information on the clipboard, the foal was a full thoroughbred, the son of Bellamy's recently deceased stud.

Yet Sam would bet her veterinary degree the mare wasn't a registered thoroughbred. She was small, and her long barrel and high hindquarters suggested quarter horse ancestry.

Curious, Sam opened the stall door and spoke gently to the mare. "Hey, sweetie. Remember me? I just want to look at your lip. I'm not going to hurt your baby…" Still crooning, Sam caught the mare's halter and inverted the horse's upper lip to reveal the shiny pink skin inside, where her racing tattoo was.

Or should have been. There was no tattoo.

The mare was either an unraced thoroughbred—in which case, why breed her to a stud with a million-dollar fee?—or she wasn't a thoroughbred at all.

"Weird." She looked at the colt again. Damned if he didn't look like a full thoroughbred, though granted it was a little tough to tell when they were that young. She let herself out of the stall as an awful suspicion formed in her mind.

The racehorse industry forbade any medical manipulation of breeding stock. Frozen semen and artificial insemination were banned, as was embryo transfer—ET. In ET, a donor mare's egg was fertilized and then implanted in a recipient mare for gestation. In the showhorse world, where it was legal, ET meant a mare could be "bred" and still remain in competition while her foal developed in another mare's womb. The technique could also be used to breed an older mare, or one that might not maintain the pregnancy. More importantly, it could allow several breedings between a mare and stallion to be born in a single season.

But ET was illegal in racehorse breeding.

Stunned, Sam moved to the next stall down, and froze when she looked at the registration numbers listed for the sire and dam of the foal within. Then she strode quickly to the next stall. The next. Then she darted across the wide barn aisle, glancing at every clipboard.

Within minutes, she'd figured out what Bellamy was up to.

There were forty broodmares in the barn with foals at their sides—but the foals came from only four different mare and stallion pairings. Bellamy had ten copies of each pairing, probably crosses that had produced winners for him in the past. Presumably, he would register the pairing under a single name, train the horses in secret and pick the fastest to run under that name. The DNA-typing required by the Jockey Club would pass with flying colors because the horse would be the true offspring of the registered parents.

But it would have been born to a surrogate and selected from among ten of its full brothers and sisters.

It was brilliant. It was also completely and utterly illegal. And who knew how long it had been going on? Who knew how many of Bellamy's wildly successful winners had been produced this way?

If the racing world ever found out, Bellamy would be ruined.

Which was why he'd paid—or simply asked—Horace Mann to kill her, Sam realized with a jolt of fear and understanding sharp enough to cause pain. He hadn't meant for the barn help to call her to the foal's birthing. Dr. Sears was no doubt neck-deep in the deception and likely performed the ET procedures himself. He wouldn't tell.

But Sam...she was Sheriff Bob's daughter. She would have blown the whistle on this illegal operation the moment she suspected. Which is why Bellamy had tried to get rid of her—for a pre-emptive strike.

And that was why he'd called her to the farm now.

To kill her.

She spun on a sudden jolt of adrenaline, then froze when she saw a man's dark silhouette framed in the sunny arch of the doors.

Before she could turn and run, he closed the distance between them, grabbed her arm, yanked it up behind her and jabbed a gun in her lower back. "Just in time for our meeting, I see, Dr. Blackwell."

Thomas Bellamy was a middle-aged man of below-average height and above-average weight, but determination and desperation lent him strength and the gun gave him leverage. He muscled Sam out of the barn and across the curiously deserted stable yard.

Heart pounding, she dug in her heels, trying to slow him, stop him, trip him up. She was frantic to do anything to keep him from manhandling her away from the farm buildings toward the paddocks and the land beyond, which ended abruptly at First Cliff, the highest of the five stone ledges that surrounded Black Horse Harbor.

Logan! Help! She instinctively shouted for him in her mind, knowing he'd come for her if he could, but also knowing he was on his way back to the city, to his life. The thought that she might never see him again speared through her, sharper even than the strain of her arm when Bellamy shoved her onto the path that led to First Cliff.

"No!" Sam screamed, hoping someone would hear

her over the rising offshore breeze. She thrashed, but couldn't budge his iron-hard grip, which pushed her inexorably toward the edge. "They know! Logan knows what you're doing. He won't let you get away with it!"

Bellamy's chuckle held little mirth. "Nobody knows except Sears and my most trusted employees, and they're all paid well for their loyalty. Don't you get it? I've been doing this for years. How do you think I breed all my winners?" He chuckled, and she wasn't sure whether he was talking to her or to himself when he said, "This is the future of racehorse breeding. Mate the best to the best over and over, cull the weaklings and race the fastest. In a few decades, I will have created an entirely new standard of thoroughbred horse. A perfectly designed, engineered animal."

"That's exactly what the Jockey Club doesn't want," Sam said, noticing that the more he talked, the more his grip on her arm slackened and the less the gun pressed into her back. "That's why they've outlawed cloning, in vitro fertilization and embryo transfers!"

"Shortsighted idiots," Bellamy snarled, his grip loosening even further. "Why can't they see that—"

Sam yanked away from him and turned to run.

"Bitch! Get back here!" He grabbed her hair and pulled her back. Sam screamed and struck out, but he looped an arm across her chest, pinning her. She kicked back, but he only grunted at the stinging contact.

Trapped! She was trapped, caged by his superior strength. By his mad greed. Tears stung her eyes and she whimpered and fought as he dragged her to the edge of the cliff. Two words reverberated in her brain.

Help me!

LOGAN'S CELL PHONE RANG as he took a country-road corner on two wheels. "Hello?"

Please let it be Jimmy calling to say she's at Jen's house, he thought. Or the sandwich shop. Anyplace but Bellamy.

But his gut told him she was at the farm.

"They've got him!" The words were what he was hoping for, since the staties were on their way to Bellamy at that very moment. But the voice was wrong.

It was female. Tearful.

"What?" he barked into the phone, conscious of time passing, of the pounding urge to reach Sam, to hold her in his arms and never let go.

"Stephen. HFH got him out. He's on his way home! He'll be here the day after tomorrow!" It was Nancy. Oh, God.

Something broke inside Logan and left him exultant and aching at the same time. Joy shivered beside terror, neither gaining the upper hand and both leaving him hollow.

He pinched the bridge of his nose and said, "That's wonderful, Nance. But I can't talk right now. Sam needs me."

And in that instant, in the moment that he put Sam ahead of his sister, he understood it. He understood that even while Nancy had sat at home, pregnant and mourning her husband while waiting for the quiet phone to ring, she hadn't regretted the marriage, or the love.

He understood it.

And so, of course, did Nancy. Her voice hitched once and she said, "Call me when you can. And take care of yourself. I love you."

"I love you, too," he said, and it was his first time speaking the actual words in a long time. "Don't worry about me, I'll be fine. I'll be there to meet Stephen's plane, I promise."

"Just make sure you and Sam are both there to meet his plane, okay?"

Logan turned between the stone pillars, blew through the parking lot and past the guard shack before the kid even knew what was coming. As he sped through the stable yard, scattering startled-looking grooms like leaves, he said, "I'm going to do my best."

He slapped the phone shut and cursed when he rounded a turn and saw two figures silhouetted against the sky. Sam and Bellamy.

Struggling at the edge of the cliff.

SAM SHOT HER ELBOW BACK and tried to ignore the pain radiating down her other arm. She'd managed to tear away from Bellamy and slap the gun from his hand. It had flown over the cliff, but at what cost? Her arm was numb from his hold, leaving her down to one fighting hand.

And two feet.

She kicked at him, missed and staggered, her balance thrown off by her bad arm. He rushed at her, arms wide as though he intended to lift her bodily and throw her off First Cliff.

The image spiked terror through her soul. *Logan! Where are you?* she cried internally, needing him even though she knew he'd be halfway to Boston by now.

Engine noise roared suddenly. Sam jerked her head toward it and saw the red pickup erupt over a low hill nearby and slide to a halt twenty feet away. Logan leaped from the truck and charged toward the edge of the cliff.

"Logan!" she cried, love and fear and joy bursting through her in a headlong rush. She reached toward him—

And Bellamy hit her with a flying tackle that sent her over the cliff.

"No!" Logan roared when he saw Sam's body fling backward and disappear over the edge. "No!"

He grabbed Bellamy by the shirt and spun the man toward the truck, away from the edge. Without giving the other man an opportunity to speak, to plead, to gloat, whatever the bastard might have thought to do, Logan sent his fist hurtling into Bellamy's face and knocked him into limp unconsciousness.

"Sam! God, Sam!" Sick with dread, with horror, with the all-but-certain knowledge that he'd figured out his priorities too late, Logan scrambled to the edge of the cliff. He lay flat on his stomach, eased his upper body over, and looked down.

And saw her.

"Logan?" Eyes wide, face pale, she perched gingerly on a ledge barely wide enough for her sneakers. Far below, the Atlantic crashed and growled around the rocks, a hungry, mindless giant waiting for its prey.

He took in the scene in a heartbeat, even as relief crashed through him, followed quickly by terror when the narrow rock outcropping crumbled beneath her left foot and pebbles fell.

She was incredibly lucky to have landed on the ledge. She'd be even luckier if it held up long enough for him to rescue her.

But it had damn well better hold up. He wasn't going to lose her now. Not when he'd just realized how much she meant to him. How much he wanted to give her and promise her.

Himself. A future.

He reached an arm down to her. "Sam, give me your hand. Gently. Just reach up and give me your hand. I'll pull you up. I swear it."

She looked up and didn't move. Her lower lip trembled, though he could see from the determination in her eyes that she was fighting the tears and the panic. "Don't you have a rope or something in the truck?"

"I do," he said, "but I don't think the ledge is going to hold out that long. Just reach up and grab. I won't let you fall. Trust me."

She lifted her hand as a few more pebbles came loose and fell, then a hand-sized chunk of rock. "I trust you.

In fact, I think I love you. I was going to tell Bellamy I didn't want the job, so we could work something out between us. But then I figured out what he's been doing…." She trailed off and looked at him, eyes dark with fear and emotion.

"You can tell me about Bellamy later," Logan said urgently. Sweat broke out across his lower back as another piece of ledge gave way. But Sam, close to shock, didn't seem to notice. So he said, "And we can talk about how we're going to make it work later, too. But the important thing is that I think I love you, too. Scratch that. I know I love you. I love you, Samantha, so *give me your damn hand this instant!*"

At his shout, she gave a little leap upward and grabbed on just as the rock beneath her feet gave way. Logan clasped his fingers tightly around her wrist, felt himself pulled a little toward the cliff, cursed and dug in with his toes and free hand. He inched backwards and felt rocks bite into his chest and stomach.

They weren't going over. No way.

He gritted his teeth at the pain in his ribs, and bodily hauled her toward the rocky edge. She used her feet to help, and gained the top quickly.

It happened in a flash. He saw her eyes widen. Heard her scream, "Logan, look out!"

Suddenly he felt himself pushed headfirst toward the drop-off.

At the last possible second, when it seemed as though gravity was sure to claim him and send him hurtling to the rocks below, Logan grabbed onto the now-conscious—and murderously angry—Bellamy and hauled himself away from the brink. The man staggered away from the cliff's edge.

Sam screamed again when Bellamy howled and lunged, and she darted forward, though Logan knew she'd be too late to save him from the villain's mad rush.

Bellamy leaped toward Logan, who pivoted aside and stuck out a foot, hoping to divert him, to bring him down shy of the brink. But Bellamy changed course and crashed into Logan, driving him to the edge of the cliff.

"No!" Sam screamed and reached for Logan. He felt rocks give beneath his feet, felt Bellamy's weight push him over—

And felt Sam's fingers close on his flailing hand.

She yanked and Logan flung himself toward safety. At the last moment, he reached back for Bellamy, but it was too late.

The racehorse breeder teetered on the edge, arms windmilling, eyes and mouth stretched wide in terror.

Then he fell, screaming.

Moments later, the screams ended with horrifying suddenness.

Stunned, shattered, and so incredibly thankful that he couldn't even put it into words, Logan turned to Sam and gathered her into his arms. For her sake. For his sake.

For their sake.

"I love you," he said into her hair. The words didn't

hurt, and they didn't create the anxiety he usually associated with knowing someone cared for him.

But this wasn't just someone. This was Sam.

She pulled away slightly to look up at him. Her eyes shone with relief and emotion. "I love you, too. We can figure out the rest as we go along."

And though that might have made him nervous, since he knew that was exactly what had gone wrong in her previous relationships, he wasn't worried. Because between them, they had more than her other relationships combined.

They had love enough to make compromises.

He dropped his head and she reached up, and their lips touched as a thunder of rotor blades, shouts and a dog's bark announced the arrival of the others.

A state police chopper set down on the flat ground downwind. Jimmy and his deputies ran up from the stable block, accompanied by half a dozen confused-looking farm employees and one mangy, yellow pit-bull cross.

Logan dropped a hand to Maverick's head and scratched the fellow behind his scraggly, scarred ears as he broke the kiss and slung his arm around Sam before turning to the others. He nodded to Jimmy. "We're okay. Bellamy's not." He jerked his head to the cliff. "It may take him a few days to wash up onshore."

Sam shivered against him, but he couldn't regret the starkness of his words. Bellamy deserved nothing more from him.

"William called," Jimmy said simply, and his eyes held a question. *Are you staying or going?* he seemed to ask. *Is it Sam or the city?*

But Logan grinned because he'd finally figured out that it didn't have to be one or the other. They'd make it be both.

He glanced at the chopper and tightened his arm around Sam. "Any way your boys could give us a ride into the city? I have some testimony to give, and I want to be there and see Trehern Sr. put away for a long, long time." He cocked his head at Sam. "You game for a day in the city, maybe a night in the penthouse? We have an airplane to meet tomorrow."

Her smile cut straight through to his soul. "They rescued Stephen?"

He nodded and grinned when she whooped a cheer and said, "I'm in."

"But Sam, what about the clinic?" Jimmy said quietly, as though offering her an out, or perhaps reminding her of something.

She reached out and linked her fingers with his, though she didn't let go of Logan. "Jen can do the small animal work. And," she glanced at the lovely farmscape, her eyes tinged with sadness, "I think we'll let the vets up north handle the large animal work, once Dr. Sears has been picked up on charges."

"Already done," Jimmy assured her, tightening his fingers. "Are you sure?"

Logan didn't step in. He waited for her to smile and

reassure her friend. "I'm sure." She turned back to him. "Shall we go?"

"Yes," he agreed, "let's."

They ducked into the helicopter together, and as the rotors sped up and the ground fell away for the trip to Boston, Logan turned to Sam and grinned. "Were you worried about me?"

"Hell, yes." She smiled back. "Were you worried about me?"

"Terrified," he admitted, though the concept wasn't as scary as it had once seemed. "Because I love you."

"Ditto." She laughed and leaned back into his arms as the chopper swung out over the sea for the trip north, where Logan would testify against Trehern, and mentally dedicate the moment to Sharilee. Then they would stand with Nancy while she welcomed her husband home.

And after that?

It would be time to build their new life. Together.

* * * * *

Coming in September 2005
watch for Jessica Andersen's gripping thriller
BULL'S EYE,
part of the five-book continuity,
BIG SKY BOUNTY HUNTERS,
only from Harlequin Intrigue!

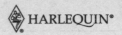

e♦HARLEQUIN.com

The Ultimate Destination for Women's Fiction

Your favorite authors are just a click away
at www.eHarlequin.com!

- Take a sneak peek at the covers and
  read summaries of **Upcoming Books**

- Choose from over 600
  author **profiles!**

- Chat with your favorite authors
  on our **message boards.**

- Are you an author in the making?
  Get advice from published authors
  in **The Inside Scoop!**

**Learn about your favorite authors
in a fun, interactive setting—
visit www.eHarlequin.com today!**